Saxon called the mark, "Wait . . . Wait . . . NOW!"

Gunnery Sgt. Mainline flipped a switch on the panel, activating the electrical ignitors that would blow the detonator caps screwed into the blocks of C-4 arranged around the roadbed.

In the near-silence, the night was rent by a bulb-popping series of magnesium-bright strobes. Moments later the rolling boom and echoes of multiple explosions rumbled across the arid landscape.

Enemy troops shouted in pain and horror as the ground gave way and they and their war machines were swallowed up by the sand, tumbling thirty feet down into the cavern where secondary explosions from the burning vehicles pulsed and thudded up into the air. The earth seemed to spit fire for a few long minutes.

Saxon barked an order, and Team Fang mounted up and bolted away from the firing line. Sgt. Mainline hollered praise to the Lord for creating the U.S. Marines. . . .

Titles by David Alexander

MARINE FORCE ONE
STRIKE VECTOR

David Alexander

BERKLEY BOOKS, NEW YORK

This is a work of fiction. Names, characters, places, and incidents either are the product of the author's imagination or are used fictitiously, and any resemblance to actual persons, living or dead, business establishments, events, or locales is entirely coincidental.

MARINE FORCE ONE: STRIKE VECTOR

A Berkley Book / published by arrangement with the author

PRINTING HISTORY
Berkley edition / January 2002

Visit our website at
www.penguinputnam.com

ISBN: 0-425-18307-6

BERKLEY®
Berkley Books are published by The Berkley Publishing Group, a division of Penguin Putnam Inc., 375 Hudson Street, New York, New York 10014. BERKLEY and the "B" design are trademarks belonging to Penguin Putnam Inc.

PRINTED IN THE UNITED STATES OF AMERICA

10 9 8 7 6 5 4 3 2 1

"We have seen [Iraq's] reconstitution of some of the infrastructure that existed prior to some of our attacks in December of 1998. What we don't know is: What is going on in those facilities? That is a cause for concern to us, given Saddam Hussein's past track record of obfus-cation and denial of his programs of WMD."

—RADM Craig R. Quigly speaking
at 1/23/01 Pentagon news conference

"We know, you beloved men and women, that the thing that hurt you most was not their aggression or their aggressive nature, but because they didn't come to meet you face-to-face, depending on a long technological arm, which is not the measure of bravery. Courage is your steadfastness, your valor and your *jihad*. So resist and fight them as we trusted you and in the same way you are known for. Fight the enemies of Allah, enemies of nation and enemies of humanity. Allah will be on your side and disgrace will be theirs, now and on the day of judg-ment."

—Saddam Hussein's statement to the
Iraqi people, 12/16/98

"You don't hurt 'em if you don't hit 'em."

—Lt. Gen. Lewis B. "Chesty" Puller,
USMC, 1962

prologue

What Is Going On at These Facilities?

chapter *one*

Major David Saxon sat behind the wheel of the fast attack vehicle, freezing his *cojones* off, the plastic-bagged handset of a SINCGARS field radio clutched in one tactical-gloved hand.

The patch on the upper right sleeve of his desert camo field jacket bore the numeral 1 on a shield surmounting the globe, anchor and rampaging eagle emblem of the U.S.M.C.

The unit's motto "Give 'Em Hell" was stitched in gold across the bottom of the patch. It was the insignia of the elite Marine Corps special operations brigade officially designated Marine Force One—the first-in, last-out force of choice for special missions too hard and too important for the other guys to handle. In fact, there wasn't another unit fit to wipe One's asses, and every Marine in the force knew it.

In addition to being cold, Saxon was exhausted, his stamina and energy almost totally spent. Marine Force

One had been on the ground too long, and the cumulative effects had begun to tell. Saxon would be pulling his personnel out. He'd just radioed HQ for an evacuation aircraft.

Three hundred miles to the southwest, inside Saudi, a V-22 Osprey convertiplane was already being prepped for takeoff at the MF-1 command center at Jauf. Another Osprey configured as a tanker would refuel the V-22 after it got airborne, and then it would be on its way to pick them up.

Too little sleep, too much adrenaline, too many Meals Rejected by Ethiopia, too much living on the edge—all of it had taken its toll on the troops. Saxon had seen evidence of combat fatigue in his personnel for the last few days, but hadn't noticed it in himself—until just before, when he'd chewed out the Marine on the other end of the radio link for no good reason, stuck the fire hose down his throat and turned on the pressure. Yeah, he was losing it. His men were losing it. It was time to get the hell out.

Saxon terminated communications with HQ and replaced the radio's handset, which was wrapped in a plastic Baggie to keep out the incredibly fine-grained powdery stuff that was less sand than moon dust.

The dust of the Iraqi desert got into everything, and was as widespread in the rocky north as the sandy south. It sifted into automotive engines, into the bolt actions of the AKMS bullpups the team carried into combat instead of the disfavored M-16—a weapon less than worthless in sustained desert ops—it even worked its way into the minute crevices of the skin. Baggies on the radio, condoms over rifle barrels; you needed this stuff here.

The sand was a hostile force, almost alive, almost part of the enemy's battle array. At its most benign it slowly enveloped the soldier in its suffocating embrace. But at times it could gather itself into the devastating storms called *shamals* by the Arabs. Such sandstorms struck without warning and always left destruction in their wake.

In the course of the nineteen consecutive days that One had been playing in the sandbox, the company-strength detachment from One's brigade-sized manpower pool had been almost devastated by one such storm. Despite an early satellite warning of the storm's approach and the hasty lashing down of their Fast Attack Vehicles, weapons and miscellaneous gear, they had been forced to spend a day digging themselves out like mummies emerging from a crypt.

Iraqi military patrols were another constant threat. MF-1 had successfully played frag-tag with enemy units out on the desert, but there'd been some damn close calls. Even with overhead coverage from UAVs and Kennan-class Improved Crystal imaging satellites, the desert's many landscape features—folds, crevices, wadis, gullies, dunes, caves, pillars, berms, dikes, canals, to name just a few—made consistently reliable intel on enemy movements impossible.

Saxon's combat savvy told him that his force's lucky streak couldn't last much longer. It was best to pull the troops out before the bovine excrement hit the whirling blades. Dead soldiers were no good to anybody—except the enemy.

Right now the desert was deceptively tranquil. Outwardly, it was another freezing night in the stony western badlands of Iraq between Basra and As Salwan. But the sector bristled with Saxon's troops, hidden away in wadis, spider holes and in seams and crevices in the landscape. In full battle dress, augmented with cold-weather gear, the forty-member Marine commando formation was deployed across a dozen miles of almost lunar desolation, tied together by secure radio and satcom links.

With Saxon in command, the formation—operationally designated B-Detachment—had been drawn from the ranks of the elite special operations brigade known variously as Marine Force One, the Big Bad One, or simply One. Some called them 1-Patchers because of their distinctive unit insignia. The detachment had been conducting special recon operations in the western desert for nearly three weeks, working in the nocturnal darkness accompanying a new moon and holing up during the day.

Tonight's mission marked the culmination of B-Detachment's patrol activities inside Iraq. B-Detachment was overdue for extraction. The rigors of conducting sustained operations in the hostile desert environment combined with the unit's dwindling rations supplies and lack of sleep alone made extraction imperative.

The detachment would have been days gone already had it not been for Saxon's determination to stay until the mission's objectives had been fully met. One had been sent into Iraq on a SLAM, or search, locate and annihilate mission. Saxon's brief had been to locate and identify the site of a plutonium refinement facility under construction in the Iraqi desert a few hundred miles to the northeast of the Saudi Arabian border.

The job had fallen to the 1-Patchers because of intelligence unearthed on One's last mission inside Yugoslavia. Saxon's mind filled with the images of fiery holocaust in the last hours of this previous campaign. Most of his original force had been killed in the confrontation with the Soviet-loaned Spetsnaz troops serving Colonel Vuc Dragunovic.

One involved party, the nameless intelligence agent— he'd used the operational alias "Congdon"—who had sent

Saxon's men to their deaths, had probably been pleased at the outcome of the mission. The intelligence haul from Dragunovic's underground lair had been a bonanza. It had pointed straight to the Middle East, where weapons of mass destruction were being manufactured. Analysis of the intelligence was why One was here now.

Saxon's thoughts jumped forward in time, to the events of the past hour, during which he had led a team inside the Iraqi installation to gather intelligence and emplace a special demolition charge to blow it up. The AH-1W Whiskey Cobra gunship that was expected in minutes would raze surface structures, including the radio and guard towers, with Hellfire missile salvos and automatic cannon strikes, but its main purpose was to create a diversion to cover the 1-Patchers' extraction by V-22 convertiplane at a nearby desert LZ.

The AH-1W stood no chance of inflicting damage to the buried portion of the deep underground facility, or DUF, which was sheathed in layers of stressed concrete and steel and impervious even to a low-yield nuclear strike. The DUF was too deep even for a B61-11 nuclear glide bomb to destroy with complete confidence in the results.

Yet a nuclear strike would, in fact, take the base down. But this would be an explosion from within, not without. Saxon and his team had penetrated the base interior and implanted an SADM, or special atomic demolition munition, at its core level.

The blast of the compact mini-nuke was calculated to shatter the foundations and implode the structure down around it, burying any residual radioactivity and hermetically sealing it beneath millions of cubic tons of rubble, wreckage and sand. Iraqi patrols that had gotten in the way had been eliminated and hidden out of sight.

Long before the bodies might have been found, the base would go the way of Sodom and Gomorrah.

Saxon's reflections were shattered by a series of hi-lo tones in his earbud.

"Magic Dog, be advised that arrival of Lynch Pin is imminent. Repeat. Lynch Pin imminent."

"That's affirm," Saxon said back. "Out."

Saxon now no longer needed the remote voice to inform him of the approach of the two aircraft. His pulse quickened as he heard the sounds that harbingered their arrival.

It began as a distant rumbling just a decibel or two above the audible threshold. Then it became a steady chugging, distorted by weird harmonics. Seconds later the two aircraft appeared as ghostly gray-white shapes in Saxon's thermal view field, the smaller, nimbler dragonfly shape of the AH-1W gunship darting in ahead of the larger, wider V-22 tilt-rotor, now in heliplane mode.

The ghost ships skimmed incredibly low across the surface of the desert, scudding like wraiths through the moonless blackness of the cold, arid night. Above the site of the Iraqi NBC installation the two ships parted company. The AH-1W took up a position several hundred yards from the base and hovered there while the V-22 broke toward B-Detachment's rendezvous point and LZ.

There was no communication from either ground or airborne personnel. Although they had secure radio links, the teams would continue to follow EMCON (emission control) procedures and maintain radio silence. Both groups had their orders, both had been briefed on the OP-PLAN, and both knew the parts they were expected to play.

The AH-1W continued to loiter low above the ground. Waiting. Waiting. Hanging and waiting.

Saxon held the wireless remote-detonation unit in one tactical-gloved hand while at the small keypad on the face of the unit he input the nuclear gold code necessary to arm and trigger the SADM, watching a line of asterisks appear on the small LED panel.

"Authorization approved," flashed the panel, a few moments later. *"Proceed to detonation countdown?"*

Saxon nodded at Top Sgt. Berlin' Hirsh who was seated beside him in the dune buggy and Hirsh put shooter's plugs in his ears. Saxon did the same.

Saxon pressed the return key.

"Detonation countdown initiated. Mark."

Saxon watched the numerals flash across the screen as the countdown sequence went from ten to zero in as many seconds. The mini-nuke was set with a backup timer in case remote detonation failed.

At the zero mark nothing happened for another second or two as the ignition processor in the dull gray steel canister chewed on stop bit number X-789B-00-5, then accepted it as valid, and began the ignition sequence. The nuke dutifully obliged, and shaped charges imploded a core of plutonium to critical mass, causing a nuclear chain reaction enriched by a tritium booster.

Saxon heard a dull rumbling beneath the earth, then felt the first shock waves radiating outward from the blast in the desert's bowels. The FAV's chassis shook and the lights around the base perimeter were suddenly extinguished.

There was no visible blast. The force of the explosion was contained and encapsulated within concrete and earth, but the concrete blockhouses, steel antenna pylons, barracks buildings, Quonset huts and other structures on the surface trembled as if struck by a severe earthquake. As they began to implode, then disintegrate, Saxon heard the shouts and screams of terrified Iraqi troops caught amid the devastation.

Their terror would be intense, though mercifully brief. At that moment, the AH-1W Whiskey Cobra began firing Hellfire missiles into the epicenter of the blast zone. Now there was flame, now there were explosions, now death strode forth from hell as a reaper of souls. As the missiles struck, seeding the earth with toadstools of flame, the gunship circled the kill zone, pouring down 20-millimeter automatic cannon fire, glowing red tracers streaking into the molten mass of burning lava to which the base had been reduced.

"Man, that was some awesome shit," Sgt. One Eyes observed.

"Top, we're out of here," Saxon told 1st Sgt. Berlin' Hirsh, and the FAV swept away into the night, toward the distant LZ, leaving a cloud of dust behind it.

Across the desert 1-Patcher personnel were breaking cover. They fell back toward the extraction LZ from hide sites and lookout posts spread out along a circular perimeter a mile in circumference.

All but one six-man team.

Team Fang remained in position on both sides of a stretch of desert blacktop. The team's orders were to remain there and cover the withdrawal of the main body of B-Detachment. Team Fang would be the last MF-1 personnel out of the op zone.

*   *   *

Saxon held onto the roll bar of the FAV as Hirsh high-balled the souped-up and heavily armed road racer across the undulations and declivities of the desert surface. Hirsh followed the track of a GPS unit that had the way-points to the rendezvous point already programmed in.

Across the desert, other teams making up B-Detachment were doing likewise. At the LZ, the V-22 had set down with its huge engine nacelles and giant paddle-blade prop-rotors tilted up in helo mode, ready for a rapid takeoff. Its rear loading ramp was lowered. Pilot and co-pilot scanned the horizon through NODs (night observa-tion devices), the copilot standing at the base of the ramp and carrying an M-249 Minimi SAW charged and fed from a 7.62-millimeter box mag, just in case things got hairy.

Mobile detachment VI of the 12th Battalion of the Hamatawli Division of the Iraqi Republican Guards was stationed at a lonely outpost in the desert not far from One's strike zone. The motorized contingent had been on a routine night patrol trawling for smugglers who had been using the route to run contraband into Jordan along the northwestern Saudi border, when it heard the rapid, pulsating booms of multiple explosions.

Its commander, Captain Ramzi Haddad, had radioed headquarters for orders and to request support. Both were immediately given. Haddad's contingent was of company strength with Haddad and three other men in a scout car and the rest of the unit in two BTR-70s, each BTR con-taining a platoon-strength element. Several of Haddad's men, including Haddad, were equipped with Belgian cop-ies of the Litton binocular M-912A night vision goggle,

Gen III class gear and the best night vision equipment the Iraqis had.

With the arrival of another company from battalion HQ imminent, Haddad judged his own small force sufficient to reconnoiter the source of the blast and issued orders to roll toward it.

If nothing else, his troops could establish an observation post near the epicenter. If it had been a military strike, they could then spot for artillery and aircrew, even other follow-on mechanized forces.

If it turned out to be an attack, his force might then play a more active role.

He was hopeful that it would be the latter.

chapter *two*

From his seat in the AH-1W Whiskey Cobra's front cockpit, the gunship's weapons systems officer or WSO (Whizzo) gazed down upon a landscape of utter devastation.

The gunner had fired off virtually every last round of ordnance the helo had carried into combat—minus a small reserve of Hellfire missiles, unguided Hydra rockets and a few thousand rounds of twenty mike-mike depleted uranium (DU) cannon rounds for the return trip back across the fence into the land of the Sheiks and the home of the rich.

Hovering several hundred yards slant-range of the target, the gunship was now lighter by nearly a ton as it hung above the burning witch's cauldron, swaying in the air as the snake driver—seated in the second cockpit above and behind the gunner's capsule—used cyclic and collective pitch controls to compensate for the powerful thermal updrafts generated by the conflagration.

The helicrew's OPPLAN called for transiting from the attack site once it had visual confirmation that the target had been neutralized, and covering the withdrawal of the Marine special forces unit in theater. The snake driver was about to beeline for the RV point when his WSO warned him of trouble.

"Moose, hold off on the transit," Marine Airman 1st Class Johnny Costanza advised over cockpit interphone, "I've just received an Urgent Arrow priority alert."

The snake driver eased back on the cyclical pitch control stick, causing the pitch of the AH-1W's dishing main rotor to change from the 30-degree cant for forward locomotion to a flat, horizontal rotation for stationary flight. At the same time he eased back on the collective to slow the revolutions of the tail boom rotor. The helo stabilized into a low hover some twenty feet above the desert crust.

Urgent Arrow was the code phrase for battlespace intelligence derived from the Tier III+ Global Hawk UAV (unmanned aerial vehicle) that had been tasked to overfly the op zone and transmit near-real-time and real-time tactical intelligence to the National Military Command Center at the Pentagon, from which the operation was remotely coordinated.

Because Global Hawk needed satellite relays to transmit the data to receiving stations on the Washington Beltway, there was a time-lag of several seconds in the Pentagon's link to the UAV. Whiskey Cobra's line-of-sight links were instantaneous, however. The WSO's console-mounted thermal scope dedicated to UAV downlink showed what the large, planelike unmanned aerial vehicle's long-range cameras were seeing from about twenty thousand feet above the battlespace.

What appeared to be a mechanized Iraqi patrol was moving across the desert toward friendly troops. The

Whizzo hit the keypad on the instrumentation panel facing him a few times to increase magnification, and nodded his head. There it was in all its glory. No question now. *Enemy*.

But he did one more thing too, and that was key IFF per international rules of engagement. Since the Gulf War's high friendly casualty rate, U.S. rules of engagement called for IFF interrogation, even with a visual confirm, unless first fired upon. As he'd known it would, IFF returned a negative confirm. The WSO keyed his mike again.

"Urgent Arrow shows two Bimps and a command vehicle approaching on Vector Bravo X-Ray Charlie Seven. I estimate we'll have 'em on thermal in thirty seconds."

"Semper Gumbi," the snake driver said back. "Let's frag them camel humpers."

"That's affirm. I'm up for it."

The snake driver pulled back on the cyclical, again canting the helo's dishing rotors into an angle some 45 degrees from the horizontal, and increased the revs to the aluminum-honeycomb and stainless-steel tail boom rotor. The AH-1W shot forward, nose slightly down, tail slightly up, in hunter-killer mode as it closed with the enemy formation.

Within a matter of minutes the Whiskey Cobra's gunner had the unfriendly patrol sighted on forward-looking infra-red. The FLIR scope presented a slant-range view of the two BMPs and an armored scout car. The helo closed fast at thirty knots but suddenly the gray-white FLIR images began to break up. The two armored personnel carriers each turned and rolled away from the contact's position on the desert, heading for the cover of nearby berms.

The Iraqi patrol had spotted the gunship and was taking evasive maneuvers.

The WSO already had one of the fleeing BTRs framed in his target acquisition reticle. He hit the joystick pickle button and the helo's onboard fire control system calculated a solution for a Hellfire strike. A heartbeat later, the helo bucked as one of the last remaining anti-armor missiles cooked off the AH-1W's left stub wing dispenser and screamed down at the target Bimp on a contrail of white smoke.

"Go, bitch, go!" shouted the WSO as the round streaked on its slanting trajectory. "Notch my gun, you sucker!"

"Impact! Impact! Good kill! Good kill!"

The night exploded as the warhead slammed into the upper glacis of the target armored vehicle, blowing a gaping, petaled hole in the steel-plate armor of the vehicle and killing most of the men inside. Those still alive spilled from the ruptured hull as the vehicle heeled over and began to snap, crackle and pop on the desert floor, sending up voluminous clouds of dense black smoke. The AH-1W's crew saw a few figures tumble from the wreckage just before the ammo and fuel stores began cooking off, creating a spate of secondary explosions.

Before the Whiskey Cobra turned to go after the surviving vehicles, the gunner turned his head to swing around the slaved M-197 autocannon beneath the first cockpit. He hit the pickle and cooked off a 16-round burst—the maximum per salvo—of depleted uranium bullets at the survivors, seeing most of them blown apart in sprays of blood, one of them cut literally in half by a fusillade across the midsection. The WSO was about to finish off the stragglers when an explosion rocked the chopper.

"Damn!" shouted the pilot. "That was close." A rocket had just gone streaking by.

And close it had been. The surviving Bimp had turned and struck back at the helo while it was busy trashing the other armored vehicle. In retaliation the BTR crew had launched a Sagger antiaircraft missile at the AH-1W. The Sagger had missed the chopper but exploded close enough to the target to box its ears.

The helo had been rocked hard by the midair detonation. Shrapnel spewed as the warhead casing's fragmentation sleeve tore holes in the gunship's main rotor and right engine nacelle, damaging sensitive propulsion systems.

Now, close behind the first, another Sagger missile streaked upward. The snake driver took immediate evasive action, jinking hard left and pulling for altitude. The incoming missile's vapor trail hissed past the cockpit canopies as the enemy warhead whooshed up into the night sky. In a moment the desert was lit up by the pulses of strobing explosions high above the sand.

Another near-miss.

Heavy tracer fire was now spurting up at the helo too, as both the scout car and the surviving Bimp opened up with their NSV 12.7-millimeter heavy machine guns, replacements for the lighter DShKs on earlier versions. The Bimp's crew was all over the desert now, taking up positions in swales and declivities on the uneven desert floor—anywhere they could find cover. Small arms and light machine gun fire soon merged with streams of bullets from the heavy MGs directed at the AH-1W.

The helo swiveled on an invisible axis in the sky as the WSO acquired the most dangerous of the two remaining vehicles, the second BTR-70 armored carrier, for a follow-up Hellfire strike. Pin flares were now being sent up from the desert floor, their hellishly flickering white phosphorous light illuminating the battlespace.

Whether deliberate or unintentional, the action on the part of the Iraqis had the effect not only of degrading the ability of the AH-1W to hide in the night and strike from cover of darkness, but also altering the helo's missile fire solution capability. The gunner's thermal sights were confused by the flares with the result that the Hellfire went dumb, slamming into the ground near the Bimp but not scoring a direct hit.

The close call left the BTR unhurt, except for shrapnel strikes on its armored skin. But the explosion did dislodge the machine gunner from his position inside the embrasure up top of the vehicle, temporarily putting the MG out of action. Turning, the AH-1W overflew the BTR, raking the nearby scout car with DU rounds. The driver and unhorsed machine gunner were killed instantly and the vehicle set ablaze.

Now the pilot hovered the AH-1W as the WSO acquired the Bimp with their last remaining Hellfire missile. He cooked it off, scoring a direct hit. The armored carrier burst into flames and began to burn up on the desert.

The helo swung around to finish off the Iraqi personnel on the ground. The spluttering light of the pin flares had died by now and infra-red targeting was once more effective.

However, as the AH-1W hunted its prey, neither the snake driver nor the WSO saw one of the surviving Iraqi troopers rise to his knees clutching a French-made Matra Mistral shoulder-fire missile launcher. Remaining at a half-crouch, the Iraqi aimed the forty-millimeter weapon, acquired the target and quickly fired.

The bird left the pipe amid a whoosh of backblast, and his comrades began to cheer as the warhead streaked toward the blind side of the helo. It struck a second later, blowing apart inside the second cockpit canopy and instantly ripping the snake driver limb from limb.

The WSO ejected, breaking his shoulder and collarbone as the explosive charges that propelled the survival capsule slammed him with crushing force against the instrumentation console. As the chute opened and he sailed down to earth, already losing consciousness, his last glimpse of the battlefield was the sight of the broken hulk of the Whiskey Cobra crashing to earth and erupting into a meteor shower of flame.

He had hardly hit the ground when the Iraqi troops began running toward the downed capsule, smashing out what was left of the cockpit glass and dragging the semiconscious airman out onto the freezing sand.

Once in the mob's hands, the leader gave the signal. The bayonets attached to the enemy's AKM rifles thrust downward again and again, until their vengeance was satisfied, until all the bayonet blades were painted with the hated one's blood. Not satisfied with this, they further desecrated the corpse by cutting off its head and booting it across the sand.

Saxon and Sgts. Hirsh and One Eyes were taking fire as they hard-charged toward the LZ, goosing the FAV to wring every last ounce of power from its overworked V-8 engine. The trio didn't know it, but they had been spotted by scouts attached to the second Iraqi patrol, a follow-on unit at full combat strength that had been dispatched to aid the smaller patrol that had called in a report on the helo strike.

Saxon punched up Urgent Arrow UAV data from Global Hawk on the integrated TRAVLER unit fitted onto the console of the vehicle. The unit had an integrated flat panel display, SINCGARS radio capability and GPS functions. Less than a minute later, the picture was clear to Saxon. The UAV showed the tactical situation in both thermal and synthetic aperture radar imagery modes.

In SAR mode, which encompassed a wider field of view than TI, Saxon was able to observe his own unit, the pursuing Iraqis and other Marine units nearby making for the LZ. The bad news was that the pursuing enemy force was a sizeable one, but the good news was that so far no hostile aircraft were in the vicinity.

Saxon keyed buttons on the milspec steel housing of TRAVLER's flat-panel display and called up a moving map display linked to GPS, showing waypoints to the LZ. He noted to his satisfaction that the dune buggy was only a short distance from the kill basket Saxon had established for just such a contingency.

In the course of the team's patrol of the area over the last two weeks, Saxon had noticed telltale cratering surrounding a stretch of desert track. From his combat experience in Mideastern deserts and in the rocky hill country of Afghanistan with the Jamiat-I-Islami mujahideen, Saxon recognized the cratering for what it was—an indication of a subterranean river that coursed beneath the desert, rising close to the surface before again plunging down into the deep layers of aquifer a few hundred yards down. The precise pathway of the part of the river close to the surface was marked by the procession of pits in a straight line that paralleled the desert roadway.

Saxon had dispatched a team to reconnoiter the largest pit, and found what he'd suspected—about thirty feet below a thin shelf of rock, there was a cavern, and at the bottom of the cavern there flowed the river he'd known would be there.

Saxon realized he had stumbled onto the perfect place to set up a kill basket on extraction, should unfriendly forces appear. The roadway went right across the roof of the cavern, and with properly placed TNT charges, the entire roadway could be blown down into the cavern in a matter of seconds, burying an entire mechanized column amid tons of rubble.

Saxon's close attention to extraction security would now pay off. He quickly cued his comms and called Team Fang manning the detonator block a few hundred yards from the sides of the roadway.

"One Zero Foxtail to Big Bear," Saxon said. "You listening?"

"Five by five," Gunnery Sgt. Mainline answered. He was crouching behind a tripod-mounted binocular TI spotter scope. Sgt. Mainline commanded a three-man team, one member of which was already warming up their dune buggies for a fast exit. "Got the frag bait on thermal."

"As soon as we pass, hit 'em, then head for the LZ."

"Hoo-ah," Sgt. Mainline said back. "They are fragged. They are history. They are smoked. Shit—I love the Marines! I wake up every morning thanking God for creating the Corps."

"Just do it, gunny," Saxon told him.

"That's a roger. Out."

Saxon hoped the gunny was as good as his bravado, for Team Fang's sake. A lot of enemy hardware was rolling toward the LZ and it was coming on fast. The extraction Osprey would be heavily loaded, even with the buggies and other field equipment left behind. The A/C would be more vulnerable to ground fire on takeoff than was normal.

Hirsch, behind the FAV's wheel, tapped Saxon on the shoulder, pointing into the night.

"Complications, *padrone*," he said.

"No shit," Saxon replied, as he saw what Hirsch meant. Complications were right.

Against the now lightening horizon danced the telltale form of an Mi-8 "Hip" helicopter. The chopper was basically a transport helo, but had limited multi-role applications—its rocket pods and, in the "E" variant, 12.7-millimeter front-mounted heavy machine gun, gave it limited offensive capability. Tonight it was plenty.

All at once the Mi-8's nose cannon opened up on the FAV. Bullets spanged off the dirt and rubble as Hirsch drove a zigzag path across the lunar terrain, the dune buggy's oversize tires keeping the wide-carriage vehicle stable at high speeds. Sgt. One Eyes jumped behind the TOW launcher mounted atop the tubular metal crash frame surrounding the top of the vehicle and got ready to counterstrike.

Sgt. One Eyes acquired the Hip in the TOW's sights and triggered the round. The wire-guided missile sped upward, hissing and spinning on its curved stabilizer fins, spooling out a black fiber-optic cable. The helo began to jink, but One Eyes trimmed attitude and course. Seconds later he had scored a kill on the chopper. It exploded in midair, raining wreckage and burning fuel slicks down on the ground.

The helo was out of commission, but the mechanized Iraqi patrol was rapidly closing with the FAV. Saxon felt the tension lessen somewhat as Hirsh highballed the small, fast vehicle across the mined section of desert road, past the concealed places where Sgt. Mainline's crew waited in ambush. From behind his thermal spotter scope, Mainline watched the Iraqi column roar into the kill basket, not suspecting that the road was mined to blow the ground out from under them.

"On my signal," Saxon said over the radio net. "Wait . . . wait . . . *Now!*"

Gunnery Sgt. Mainline flipped a switch on the main control panel, activating the electrical ignitors that would blow the detonator caps screwed into the blocks of C-4 arranged in a rough rectangular pattern around the road-bed. Mainline had checked the circuits twice and once again. He was sure everything was good to go. He wasn't proven wrong by events.

In the near-silence, the night was rent suddenly by a bulb-popping series of magnesium-bright, quick-pulsating strobes. Light travels faster than sound, and the explosions still had to earn their miles. Moments later the rolling boom and echoes of multiple explosions rumbled like thunder across the arid landscape.

Enemy troops shouted in pain and uncomprehending horror as the ground supporting them gave way and they and their war machines were swallowed up by the sand, tumbling thirty feet down into the cavern where secondary explosions from the burning vehicles boomed and thudded violently up into the rain of falling rubble. For a few long minutes the earth seemed to be vomiting up its fiery guts.

When the fireworks died down, and the screams of the dying subsided, Team Fang mounted up their FAVs and bolted away from the flaming havoc they had unleashed upon the enemy.

Sgt. Mainline hollered praise to the Lord for creating the U.S. Marines, and this time nobody was around to stop him.

Saxon and his crew arrived at the LZ to find that most of his units had already boarded the Osprey. Others still on the ground were busily stripping classified gear from their vehicles, carrying what they could take with them onboard, and blowing the rest with demo charges.

Saxon's team gathered up code books, personal gear and weapons, and tossed grenades into the FAV. The explosions in the night would give their position away, but their situation was compromised anyway by now.

The V-22 pilot leaned out the flight deck window, waving Saxon over.

"Let me know when we can take off, sir, and we're out of here."

"Won't be long, captain."

The convertiplane's twin engines were upturned in helicraft mode, the rotors spinning and the engine warm. The multimode transport was ready for immediate dustoff.

Saxon took a head count. Only Sergeant Mainline's Team Fang was missing. Where the hell were they?

The sudden sound of approaching vehicle engines made those standing guard train their weapons in its direction. Saxon looked out into the night and lowered the barrel of his AKMS. It was the last FAVs with the four Team Fangers inside them.

"Shake your asses," he shouted at the latecomers. "Grab your gear and blow the rest. You know the drill."

"Yes, sir!" Sergeant Mainline yelled back. "Man, I love the Marines! Shit, the Marines are better than any pussy I ever got. Every day's a good day in the Marines. Every night's a party. May God bless the Corps!"

The team knew the drill backward. Within two minutes time the FAV was a burning hulk and its former passengers had joined the rest of B-Detachment inside the waiting Osprey.

"Come on, get jiggy with it," Saxon shouted at the pilot, who flashed him the OK sign. The V-22's copilot immediately raised the rear hatch and the convertiplane ascended straight up into the night.

Flying nap of the earth, ten minutes off the LZ, the tilt-rotor aircraft took fire from something out on the desert, but it was now moving too fast to be accurately taped by small arms bursts and there was no more incoming after that.

Only when they returned to Jauf did ground maintenance crew notice the pattern of bullet punctures just inches from a critical part of the Osprey's left engine nacelle. In the end it had been a closer call than anybody had realized.

book one

Now and on the Day of Judgment

chapter *three*

At the Berlin bureau headquarters of the Weisbaden-based German Federal Criminal Police Agency, the *Bundeskriminalamt*, otherwise known by the acronym BKA, which is the rough (but by no means exact) equivalent of the American FBI, they called Helmut Mauthner "Starsky" and his partner Karl Voss "Hutch." The two cops cultivated the association—Mauthner was a Bavarian with the dark hair, ruddy face and swarthy build of a mountain gnome, while Voss, whose lineage was Tyrolean, had blond hair and a fair complexion—earning a reputation for playing it fast and loose on the job.

Today, on a windswept day in early October, with Mauthner behind the wheel of a blue Volkswagen Golf and Voss slouched in the passenger seat with his sneaker-shod feet propped on the dash, the cops were sitting on a stakeout on a residential street between the Pariser Platz and the left bank of the Spree River. It was a neighborhood of cheap housing that had sprung up from the

rubble-strewn wasteland formerly in the shadow of the
Berlin Wall. Since the influx of refugees from the East
after unification, the neighborhood had become a magnet
for Berlin's growing population of foreign immigrants
from the Balkans, Eurasia and the Middle East.

For the most part, and despite periodic outbreaks of
neo-Nazi skinhead violence, the denizens of the quarter
lived harmoniously. But civil unrest and ethnic tensions
were not what had brought Starsky and Hutch to the
neighborhood. They were one team in three that was staking out a group of new arrivals to the vicinity. These
newcomers had been brought to the attention of the BKA
when a kilo-weight package of Semtex plastic explosive
had been discovered by a DHL courier making a shipment
to a neighborhood grocer when the shipping carton had
accidentally opened before delivery.

Checks with Immigration and Interpol had disclosed
that the grocer's cousin, a man named Farouk Al-Kaukji,
had recently arrived from Damascus, Syria, and was stay-
ing on a thirty-day visitor's visa. Al-Kaukji, who was
missing his right arm and part of his right leg, had a history with Interpol that went back several years. Thus he
had been watchlisted at Tempelhof Airport and the BKA
notified of his arrival. Al-Kaukji was a bomb-maker for
the radical faction of Islamic revolutionaries led by former
PLO and Black September leader Dr. Jubaird Dalkimoni.

Dalkimoni, who had long since broken with his early
affiliations and become a free agent called Abu Jihad, had
employed Al-Kaukji's services on several occasions, especially in bombs used to down jetliners, a specialty of
Al-Kaukji's. The combination of Al-Kaukji and a kilo of
Semtex added up to the possibility that Berlin was once
again becoming a major terrorist bomb assembly entrepot.

Chief of Counter-terrorist Operations at the Berlin

bureau of the German BKA, Inspector Max Winternitz, had ordered a team to put the grocery under twenty-four-hour surveillance. Another team began following Al-Kaukji as he emerged from the grocery and went about his daily rounds.

On the first day of the stakeout, the BKA team positioned behind the window of an Indian restaurant across the street from the grocery saw a late-model black Mercedes sedan pull up in front of the store. The Mercedes was driven by a stocky, goateed man who was later identified as one Farid Housek, a naturalized German originally from the Egyptian capital city, Cairo.

Housek had no record with Interpol, Europol or the BKA's INPOL or SIS criminal database systems, but the FBI knew a little about him from the high-rolling days of BCCI. Housek had then been a minor bagman for the Bank of Credit and Commerce International's Bonn headquarters, used as a go-between in arms transfer deals. With the collapse of BCCI in the late 1980s, Housek had taken a job in the accounting department of Iran Airlines and had led a mostly clean life. Until now, that is.

A tail team had followed Al-Kaukji in the company of Housek to various destinations around town, most of which were to make purchases at a miscellaneous assortment of shops. At a large department store, Al-Kaukji inspected a number of alarm clocks, and bought four of them. At a computer dealer, Al-Kaukji came out with a laptop and was found to have ordered a desktop PC for delivery to the grocer's for the following day. Other items included a pair of stereo jam boxes, batteries, wire, a portable drill of Japanese manufacture and an assortment of screws, tools and other miscellaneous odds and ends.

Housek not only chauffeured Al-Kaukji around Berlin, but also brought the bomb-maker to other stops where they met with groups of other men, all of them of Middle Eastern nationality, and all but one of them with known links to fundamentalist and Islamist terrorist organizations.

I n the gray Toyota van parked a half block down the street from Housek's apartment building in the more prestigious Gneisenau section of Berlin, the stakeout team had just started on the first round of coffee and danishes. The van was linked by spread spectrum cell communication and secure radio to each other and to the BKA's headquarters at 24 Leipsigerstrasse. Max Winternitz had just taken a call from Gerhardt Fromm, leader of the stakeout team.

Today was an important day. Winternitz had been about to give the order for the teams to move in and make arrests when a tap on Al-Kaukji's phone at the grocer's revealed that Abu Jihad himself, Dr. Jubaird Dalkimoni, was expected to personally supervise operations in Berlin.

Dalkimoni had entered the country under an official government passport issued by the Iraqi Ministry of Religious Affairs, but had been identified by a sharp-eyed BfV (*Bundesampt für Verfussungsschutz* or Office for the Protection of the Constitution) internal security watcher who scanned airport videotape footage.

The phone tap had yielded a reference to the "cakes" that had arrived and how important it was to "bake them just right." Winternitz decided to postpone the bust until Jihad was in the area.

Winternitz heard Fromm on the other end of the line.

"Blower just arrived in a cab."

"Blower" was the code name Winternitz's teams used to refer to Dalkimoni. "He's just paid the driver. Now heading up the walk and entering the building."

"Keep him in sight. Don't lose him," Winternitz instructed his men. "I'll be right over."

Winternitz grabbed his jacket and dropped the cell phone into his coat pocket. It was not usual for the Chief of Counterterrorist Operations to be in on an impending bust, but this was different.

For one thing, Winternitz had a personal score to settle with Abu Jihad. He wanted to be in on the bust when it went down. In fact, he intended to collar Dalkimoni himself. It was a promise he'd pledged to keep five years before.

The black Mercedes SL pulled up to the curb with a screech of tires. Winternitz was out the door even before the driver had shifted into park. He looked once at the entrance to the apartment building on Marskberger-strasse and then toward the van.

Inspector Buckholz, Fromm's second in command, had crossed the street toward the big boss.

"Are Blower and Oyster still inside?"

"Affirmative," Buckholz answered. "We have a laser detector on the window. We're listening to them in Oyster's living room right now."

Winternitz turned to one of the two men from the SL's backseat.

"Go around the back, make sure there are no other ways out of the place. Find the superintendent if necessary," Winternitz told them, adding, "I don't want any slipups, understood?"

"Don't worry, Boss, there won't be any," said Rudy, the shorter of the two, and he motioned for the other man to join him. Winternitz watched the two raincoat-clad figures cross the street to the building's entranceway.

To Buckholz he said, "Take three men from your team
and cover the front of the building. Hans and I are going
in the front as soon as Rudy and Rolf secure their end."

Buckholz nodded. Turning his back to the front of the
building and pulling his police radio from his pocket, he
began walking across the street. Winternitz leaned against
the Mercedes and lit a cigarette. He'd been trying to quit
for weeks but this was one occasion when he desperately
needed a smoke.

Housek looked at the bullpup automatic rifle propped
against the wall like it was something from another
planet. Dalkimoni caught the look that told him what
Housek didn't dare voice to the bomb-maker: that he was
not a man accustomed to using the weapons he occasion-
ally dabbled in selling, and that the realization that he was
in way over his head had suddenly dawned on him like
thunder.

"Don't crap out on me, Housek," Dalkimoni advised
the other man with icy disdain, not failing to notice the
beads of sweat standing on his forehead. "If necessary,
you will use that to cover my escape."

He nodded toward the weapon.

"Don't worry. I'm OK," Housek assured him.

Dalkimoni doubted this seriously. But he had no other
choice than to depend on the coward for backup.

They had made the cops staking out the building earlier
that morning. They knew a bust was coming down. While
the cops' laser bug monitored a tape recording Dalkimoni
had made earlier, of casual conversation inside the safe
house Housek kept, they had broken out the guns.

Dalkimoni cocked the bolt action on the AK-47 assault
rifle he cradled, jacking a 7.62-millimeter round into the

firing chamber. It was almost showtime. He looked toward the rear window and licked his lips.

Winternitz stole a glance at his wristwatch. He'd given his three stakeout teams watching Al-Kaukji's friends in other neighborhoods enough time to get into position. *Enough.* He picked up the Philips shortwave commo unit and hit the squelch.

"This is Winternitz to all teams. Team One, ready?"

A moment later two hi-lo tones came from the hand-held's speaker followed by Hutch's voice.

"Ready to go, Chief."

"Team Two, what is your situation?"

"We're in position outside Canker's—Al Kaukji's—apartment block," the cop named Bermann reported. "We're ready as soon as the girl with big tits walks by and Helmut shoves his eyeballs back in their sockets."

"This is not a party," Winternitz told the cop on the other end. "You're not being paid to fuck around. Get in position."

"Sorry, Chief," Bermann said sheepishly. "Don't worry. *Alles ist in ordnung*—Everything's in order."

"It had better be."

Winternitz said no more. He was in no mood to be trifled with. His men knew very well that their usually easygoing chief was keyed up on this bust. Each had to admit that in Winternitz's position, their nerves would also have been on edge.

"Rolf, Rudy—are you gentlemen in position?" he asked the two men he'd sent around back of the apartment block, the other half of the third bust team.

"All in order," Rudy's voice came back.

"Then it's a go," Winternitz told all the teams. "Repeat.

It's a go. I don't want any heroics, just good, clean police work. *Viel glück zum allen.* Good luck to you all. Winternitz, out."

The BKA chief clipped a photo ID card to the breast pocket of his navy blue topcoat and worked the action of his Sig-Sauer P226 9mm semiautomatic pistol. He slipped the gun in his right coat pocket, gestured to Hans and crossed Marksbergerstrasse toward the building's entrance.

L ess than five miles to the east, on a street in the Mittel district, the blond girl with the breasts like helium-filled balloons tipped with Chianti corks, who had simultaneously given Helmut eyestrain and *"der Ständer"*—a hard-on—was frantically explaining to a bearded man that they had been burned.

"I made them as cops," she told Farook Nasser, one of the three other men in the flat, all of whom had been part of another cell of Al-Kaukji's bomb-making terrorist brigades in Berlin.

"You're seeing cops in your sleep, Nikki," Nasser told the buxom blond woman. "You're smoking too much hashish, I think. Probably fucking too much also. It's making you paranoid."

"I fuck men for a living. I smoke hash for fun. But I'm not paranoid," Nikki replied, miffed. "I know they're cops because I recognized the one who was ogling me," she told him, straining to appear calm. "He used to work vice when I strolled the Ku'Damm two years ago. My hair was dark then. He doesn't remember me, but I recognized him. He's a filthy pig, that one, a real *tittengrapscher*. Liked to feel up the girls—sometimes worse."

The three men eyed each other. Al-Kaukji nodded at

Nasser. Maybe the bitch wasn't as paranoid as they thought after all. Best to take precautions. Al-Kaukji spoke a few words in rapid street Arabic to his companions. Each went to grab and charge his weapon.

Starsky Mauthner rapped on the closed door of the grocery. There was no answer. He gestured to his blond-haired partner to try the basement door. There was no answer there either. Since they both had probable cause, they decided to try to kick the main door in. Also, the door looked fairly easy to smash. "Eminently kickable" was Mauthner's term.

A few heel-and-sole boot smashes later, the two cops were hustling inside in half-crouches, weapons drawn. They found Al-Kaukji's cousin cowering in a corner of the room. He didn't give them any trouble as he was cuffed and read his constitutional rights under German federal law. They found a back room and the grocer let him in.

Mauthner gave out a low whistle. They had found something really interesting in here.

Winternitz walked up the service stairs; a sign on the ground-floor elevator said that the lift was out of service. Oyster's flat was on the fifth and top floor of the apartment block and Winternitz had three more flights left to go. He was already beginning to get winded. It was those damned cigarettes, that and the creeping effects of the aging process.

He'd been a cop for twenty-four years already, and he had another six years to go before becoming eligible for retirement, four if he opted for early retirement. Perhaps

he would, after all, especially if . . . but he dared not let
himself complete the thought. It might interfere with the
job ahead. Winternitz was by no means a superstitious
man, but after tragedy strikes and logic is proven wrong,
superstition tends to creep in.

Some five years before, Winternitz's only child, his
daughter Juliana, had been a flight attendant on a Lufthansa flight out of Abu Dhabi, Saudi Arabia, bound for
the Caspian seaport of Riga, Finland. An hour into the
five-hour flight, when the plane had reached its cruising
altitude of 30,000 feet over the Barents Sea and the captain had turned off the seat belt and no smoking signs, a
group of Islamic terrorists armed with rifles and grenades
had seized control of the cabin and cockpit.

The episode followed the pattern of so many others that
had taken place since the first early airline hijackings by
the PLO faction Black September in the early 1970s. In
the end a strike by *"Die Lederkopfen"*—the German
counterterrorist strike force GSG-9—had ended a standoff
on the tarmac of Helsinki International Airport.

No passengers were killed in the hijacking; in fact there
was only one friendly casualty. This was Winternitz's
daughter. She had died long before the *Lederkopfen*—
Leatherheads—took the plane.

Juliana was killed while trying to stop the brutal beating
of an American onboard the plane. The man's passport
had borne what the terrorists had thought was a Jewish-
sounding name. This and the fact that he had been carrying military papers provoked their ire.

No one had raised a finger while two hijackers
punched, kicked and pistol-whipped the passenger. Juliana
could finally stand it no longer, and despite the risks to
her own personal safety, she intervened.

She received a bullet in the heart for her trouble. She

had died almost instantly, but her efforts probably saved the life of the victim.

The American was one of the survivors. But Juliana, Winternitz's beloved daughter, had returned home in a pine box. Winternitz was shattered by the news and embittered when the man who had pulled the trigger was found to have escaped before the commando raid commenced.

He was later identified as a man named Dr. Jubaird Dalkimoni, a Palestinian from Gaza whose first career had been as a veterinarian—thus the "Dr." title—with ties to several terrorist groups.

Dalkimoni had dropped out of sight for years, then reappeared. By now he was an *éminence grise* among younger terrorists and dubbed by the honorific title of Abu, or uncle.

Jubaird Dalkimoni, murderer of Max Winternitz's daughter Juliana, was Abu Jihad, the man Winternitz had come here today to arrest.

Two floors above them, inside apartment number 5-11, as Winternitz and Hans trudged up to the landing of the apartment block's third floor, Jubaird Dalkimoni had pried from a section of kitchen wall the last corner of a roughly four foot square sheet of heavily enameled galvanized aluminum framed by strips of plywood, between the refrigerator and the ornate prewar molding that surrounded the kitchen entrance.

It had not taken Dalkimoni long to work the flat blade of the screwdriver beneath the seam of the rectangle, which had been painted in high-gloss white to match the wall in which it was set.

The emergency exit from the apartment had been Farid

Housek's idea. He had noticed the frame when he had moved in the previous year. Because the building dated back to before the Second World War, Housek suspected that the frame was a patch put in to cover what had once been the door of a dumbwaiter shaft.

Since the apartment was about to be repainted anyway, Housek had decided to pry the panel loose and see what was behind it. As he'd suspected, the musty-smelling shaft stretched all the way down, ostensibly to the basement.

More surprising, the dumbwaiter itself was still in place, just over his head, moored there probably since the end of the Hitler era. Housek pulled on the heavy chain and lowered the dumbwaiter, finding it still in sound working condition.

Farid Housek decided that it might be useful in the event he needed to make a hasty getaway sometime. He spent the better part of a day testing to see if it would reliably support his weight. This it did, and Housek was in fact able to lower himself all the way down to the basement. Satisfied, he replaced the panel and had not touched it since the painters had come. But he had been incautious in blurting out his secret to Dalkimoni shortly after his arrival.

This had been a mistake. It was now Dalkimoni who had commandeered the dumbwaiter escape route to save his own neck. Housek was ordered to remain behind and sacrifice his life if necessary to cover Dalkimoni's escape. Adnan Khadouri, fanatically devoted to the cause, was left behind to insure that Housek's loyalty and dedication did not falter.

"*Allah akbar!* God is great," Khadouri said to Dalkimoni as his leader stepped cautiously inside the narrow shaftway and placed one foot on the dumbwaiter. "Don't worry, my brother. We'll give you plenty of time to get away."

"Make sure I have at least five minutes," Dalkimoni curtly replied, climbing entirely into the dumbwaiter and crouching atop the shelf.

Khadouri blessed his boss again and resealed the opening with the now somewhat dented panel. Then he cocked the AK-47 cradled in his hands and went into the living room.

Farid Housek was sitting on the couch, his head propped between his palms, his body shivering. Clearly, he was a man without heart, a craven coward. Worse yet, in Khadouri's eyes Housek was a *mahmoon*, he who takes it up the ass.

Adnan Khadouri got the assault rifle from where it leaned against the wall and tossed it on the couch beside the gutless Housek. He told this spineless *mahmoon* to pick up the rifle and prepare to die like a man.

At that moment, Winternitz and Hans were reaching the landing of the fifth floor and crossing toward the apartment door with pistols drawn.

Winternitz took up a position to one side of the metal door frame. Hans crouched near the stairway landing, out of the direct line of sight of the eyehole at the center-top of the entrance door. Both cops' Sig-Sauer semiautomatic pistols were drawn and charged with a round in the chamber.

Winternitz held his gun in one hand while he reached out to rap on the door with the other. Hans clutched his weapon in a two-handed combat grip, his body planed sideways toward the door and his right eye lining up the twin white dots of the rear U-sight with the single red dot

of the front sight in a direct line with the door at approximately the chest height of anyone who might open it.

Winternitz rapped on the door and waited a second or
two. No answer came in response. He quickly glanced at
Hans and tried again.

"Police!" he shouted. "*Aufmachen!*—Open the door.
We have a warrant to search the flat!"

Both cops could now hear the telltale clink of eyehole
covers to the left, right and behind them being slid aside
as occupants of the floor looked out to see what all the
commotion was about.

One door at the corner opened a crack. Winternitz held
up his shield and gestured at the woman in curlers and
housecoat. The door quickly shut again, and he could hear
the security chain ratchet into place.

Winternitz prepared to rap a third time.

A volley of automatic fire punched through the thin
sheet metal skin covering the original hardwood door. The
rapid series of pops echoed through the tiled hallway, the
steel-jacketed bullets fragmenting as they ricocheted off
walls, floor and stairway.

Winternitz knew he should call in the SWAT team at
this point, but he was not about to step back and let some
hot-shit heroes grab his collar. Let them sack him if they
wanted. This was his bust or nobody's.

Winternitz had signed out a door-blowing charge from
Ordnance and brought it with him, knowing it might come
in handy. The small C-4 cutting charge was designed to
clamp over the lock plate. Winternitz quickly put it in
place, shouted a final warning and took cover.

As the C-4 detonated, the door blew in, coming right
off the hinges and falling flat on the floor of the apartment's foyer. Hans charged through, tossing in two flash-
bangs, one after the other, just to make sure.

The two cops were in after the nonlethal grenades went off with loud noise and blinding, disorienting flashes.

Adnan Khadouri was on his feet, pointing the business end of an AK right at them. Triggering the rifle he blind-fired a multiround burst, striking Hans square in the chest. Hans went down with a groan of pain and Winternitz fired back, catching Khadouri in the upper chest and face area with a salvo of 9-millimeter hollowpoints.

As Khadouri's upper torso exploded into a raw ham-burgerlike mass, Farid Housek flung aside his weapon. He was dazed and disoriented from the effects of the flash-bangs, but he knew that he was not about to die for any-body's bullshit revolution. Not even for Allah.

Winternitz slapped the cuffs on Housek and then cau-tiously scoped out the apartment with pistol drawn and a fresh high-capacity clip in the mag well. Dalkimoni was nowhere in sight.

The chief returned to Hans and found that he was still alive. The Kevlar vest under his coat had absorbed the impact of the bullets. Though Hans was grimacing in pain, it was probably a combination of shock trauma and sev-eral broken ribs. If a lung wasn't punctured, he'd be back at work in two weeks.

Winternitz called for an ambulance for Hans on his handheld radio and took another look around the apart-ment. In the kitchen he noticed chips of old enamel paint littering the floor.

It took him another second or two to pry loose the wall panel and understand what had happened.

Inspector Helmut Offenbach was surprised when the busty *mädchen* he'd earlier seen on the street opened the door in response to his knock and his shouted identification as a police officer. She smiled innocently and told him she was alone in the apartment, and that they must have the wrong place.

Helmut insisted on taking a look around anyway, but he had momentarily dropped his guard. Nikki had come to the door wearing only a sling bra and low-cut panties, and there was little left to the imagination, including the platinum blonde's incongruously dark bush. As he entered the apartment, a bearded man with unkempt black hair popped up from behind a sofa and fired a shotgun blast. At only a few yards distance most of the fan of thirty-ought-six steel balls caught Helmut in his upper torso.

Enough of the pellets hit beyond the zone of protection afforded by his bulletproof vest. A butterfly of five of them was enough to tear away most of his throat, including his larynx and the lower third of his trachea. Helmut spouted a plume of blood and reached toward his mangled throat as though trying to stuff the flaps of hanging flesh and bulging masses of blood pudding back into it as the impact hurled him against the wall.

Outside in the hall, his partner Adolph Bermann heard the shotgun blast and the shrill woman's scream that followed it. He knew better than to try and bull his way inside the flat. Instead he retreated down the stairs and radioed for reinforcements. The routine bust had turned sour in a hurry.

This was not turning out to be a very good day, now was it? He thought sourly.

By the time the medics arrived, Winternitz was out the apartment door in a sweat. He shoved past them full-tilt to the edge of the landing.

"*Wohein?*" he shouted aloud. "Where?"

He meant where did Blower/Dalkimoni go, where could he hope to find the bastard before he slipped away for good?

Getting stares but no answer, Winternitz raced down the steps and out into the street, thankful for the force of gravity that made it much easier on the way down than it had been climbing up to the fifth floor.

"What happened up there?"

It was Rudy, one member of the stakeout team from the back. Winternitz had forgotten all about the two men he'd placed there.

"Blower got away," Winternitz told them. "He had a back way out. Through the basement. But he's still got to be somewhere close. Fan out. Cover the neighborhood. Be damned careful."

"Right, Chief," Rudy said, he and Rolf already in motion.

Winternitz began running toward the street corner. But it was useless, he knew. Dalkimoni had outwitted him. He should have had a team of fucking *Lederkopfen* hit the place from all sides—helicopters, APCs, the whole works. But there was no point in blaming himself. Felons sometimes evaded the tightest dragnets.

The cop slowed to a lope as he moved through pedestrian traffic on the avenue, his eyes tiredly scanning the gathering crowds for any sign of his quarry.

Suddenly Winternitz saw the dark-haired man crossing the street near the corner of Furstenstrasse, a half block down, right by the U-bahn, the subway station entrance. It was only a fleeting glance from a sizeable distance, but Winternitz was hit by a gut feeling. He began running toward the man who, sighting him in pursuit, turned suddenly and then began running himself, racing pell-mell through rush-hour traffic toward the subway entrance.

Winternitz didn't care if he had a heart attack. His entire being, body and soul, was fixed on catching up with the perp he'd just glimpsed.

Fortunately, the heavy traffic was making it hard for the escaping terrorist to cross to the other side. Cars were honking and drivers shouted at him as he made for the U-bahn entrance. Winternitz held up his badge at an irate motorist and continued to give chase to the perp.

Dalkimoni hotfooted it down the concrete steps, shoving commuters out of the way in his haste to evade pursuit. Winternitz reached the top of the stairs seconds later. A crowd of passengers just disembarked from an arriving train were now rushing toward him up the steps. Despite his detective's ID, Winternitz had to fight them to the mezzanine level at the foot of the stairway.

Directly ahead, he now saw a maze of passenger tunnels, three of them branching off in different directions. The cop ran to the center tunnel and spotted a man running along it about twenty yards dead ahead. Winternitz took off after him. Putting on a final burst of speed that he feared would burst his overtaxed heart, he finally closed within shouting distance of the perp he'd chased to ground.

"Abhalten!" he cried out. *"Polizei!"*

But the man kept on booking and wouldn't stop. Ignoring the pursuing cop he knocked passengers out of the way, emptying his pockets on the run. Winternitz gave chase and finally caught up with his quarry after another brief sprint.

With his last remaining reserves of strength, the cop launched a flying tackle at the perp, managing to lock his arms around his calves and bringing him down to the hard floor of the subway tunnel.

Now both men went sprawling onto the concrete, Winternitz landing on top of the smaller, slimmer man. Fueled by adrenaline, Winternitz pulled out his spare cuffs and secured the suspect's wrists behind his back. He turned him over and immediately knew something was wrong.

The man was not Blower. He had fucked up. The scars on his arms marked him immediately as a junkie, probably an immigrant from Turkey or Morocco who had brought his habit with him and was spreading it around in his adopted homeland. Glassine envelopes, crack vials and drug works littered the dirty floor of the subway tunnel like bread crumbs from a fairytale.

The bomb-maker had given him the slip. Winternitz had collared himself *ein Rottler*—a two-bit hype.

On the S-Bahn elevated express to which he had transferred from the U-Bahn heading toward the commuter lines servicing the Leipsig rail junction, Dr. Jubaird Dalkimoni stood grasping a handhold in the center of the crowded passenger train. He kept his face turned toward the advertising placards above the windows. Though he was sure he was safe, there was no sense in breaking tradecraft. Ever.

At the next stop, he got off, switched to another S-bahn line, rode it three more stops, and then went up to street level amid the crowd of emerging commuters.

There, at the kiosk on the corner, he spotted a municipal transit bus arriving. The terrorist went onboard and paid his fare. He knew that the bus was going in the general direction of one of the safe houses maintained by G.I.D., Iraq's intelligence service, and he had been given emergency passcodes to gain acceptance and aid from other cells if the operation went sour.

That was all, for the moment, that he needed to know.

chapter *four*

It was ten A.M. in the Berlin Tiergarten. Max Winternitz sat feeding the pigeons that clustered around his legs, cooing and pecking.

There was an aging hippy who sold postcards, souvenir knickknacks and bags of seed at one of the entrances to the sprawling park, and Winternitz was in the habit of buying a bag from him for half a deutsche mark. He'd seen him there for years, a fixture of the park as much as the trees were.

Winternitz liked the pigeons. Though they squabbled and pecked at one another, he'd never once seen them draw blood. Less could be said about human beings.

A week had passed since the bust of Farouk Al-Kaukji and his bomb-makers, and still the main actor, Jubaird Dalkimoni, was nowhere to be found. Unofficially, Winternitz had strong reason to believe that he had made good his escape and was now safe in Iraq. Officially, though, the Arab terrorist chieftain was still at large.

Winternitz knew better. At the same time, the scum that his cops had rounded up in the raids were vanishing into the ground like earthworms.

One by one, their lawyers were getting them released on various legal pretexts. Insufficient evidence, improper search and seizure—any legal dodge seemed to suffice.

The Lockerbie bombing investigation, and the U.S.-instigated extraditions and trials that had ensued, had subjected European governments to outside pressures from all sides that they would rather not see repeated in any way.

The word had come down from Bonn—no one was to be tried. The problem was to be made to simply evaporate. And one other thing: The Americans were to be kept out of the picture.

Winternitz was in the Tiergarten to do just the opposite. Let them sack him if they liked. Not that they would.

There were factions in the BKA that were pro- and anti-CIA. Winternitz was representing a circle that was friendly to U.S. intelligence and formed a nucleus of backchannel sources from inside the German intelligence and police establishments.

Winternitz flung the last handfuls of millet seed at the moving mass of gray, brown and white feathers on the octagonal cobbles of the pavement. When he looked up he saw a man approaching down one of the walks.

Winternitz lit a cigarette. Continuing to toss handfuls of seed to the pigeons which cooed noisily as they pecked it off the cobbles, he studied the man with a feigned casualness perfected over a lifetime of police work.

Major David Saxon took a seat beside Winternitz on the park bench and sat watching the pigeons pecking at their lunch. He'd been briefed on the meet by the spook Congdon—the same Congdon who had ordered the team

into combat to destroy a classified black box a few months
before, or at least one claiming to be the same intelligence
agent.

Saxon recognized Winternitz from the three-position
Bertillon intelligence photo he'd been shown. He'd been
told that the cop would be feeding the pigeons. Well, here
he was, birds and all.

Saxon went through the rest of the procedure.

"So many birds," Saxon said in German, in which he
was fluent from years of living in the country. "You must
be wealthy to feed them these days."

He didn't like Berlin anymore. Germany had been a
pressure cooker, the U.S. military establishment all
fucked-up with petty politics. If Desert Storm hadn't come
along, Saxon figured he'd have probably wound up frag-
ging a brass hat, maybe two.

"Not too many, really," Winternitz replied. "And, besides, it calms my nerves."

"Mr. Saxon, I presume," Winternitz added, switching
over to English. "We shall sit here a minute longer while
I finish up this bag of seed. Then you will get up, bid me
auf wiedersehen and walk toward that park entrance just
ahead. Karl, one of my men, is waiting in a gray Audi.
He will drive you directly to a safe house my office main-
tains. I shall arrive separately a short while after your
arrival. Any questions, Mr. Saxon?"

"None," Saxon replied.

A few minutes later he was standing and waving *auf
wiedersehen*, then walking toward the park entrance. Winternitz turned his attention back to the birds, scattering
seeds until the bag was empty. Then he too got up and
left.

*   *   *

In the basement of BKA headquarters on Friedrich-strasse, a police clerk named Joachim Kneble sat inventorying the evidence seized during the counterterrorist raids. The evidence was heaped across a row of three trestle tables stacked end-to-end against a wall of the basement storage area.

Behind Kneble stretched a square reinforced concrete chamber that was half the size of a football field and contained row upon row of battleship-gray steel shelves, most of which bulged with evidence seized during various police actions. Directly in front of Kneble was the black cabinet of a Blaupunckt stereo receiver.

Kneble was a stereo buff and the receiver was a newer model than the Blaupunckt Kneble owned. In fact he recalled having just learned from the Web that this particular model had replaced his own, which had been discontinued. This group of factors proved to be a fatal combination. Kneble couldn't resist at least fiddling with the knobs and buttons on the face of the squat black box.

Sigfried "Siggie" Sonntag was phoning in an order for delivery at the local Thai take-out place for himself, his partner Freidrich "Fritzl" Ettinger and one of the sergeants on the night shift who was just leaving, when the light flashed on the other phone line. Sonntag quickly signed off and took the call, automatically tensing. It was a quarter past ten in the morning and nobody phoned the BKA's ordnance disposal unit at this hour unless it was a serious matter.

Sonntag slid a notepad across the chipped black paint of the metal desktop to the phone and penciled notes onto the ruled paper. By this time his partner had come up behind him and was looking over his shoulder as he hastily wrote. Sonntag concluded the conversation and hung up the phone.

Ettinger had grasped most of it from what he'd seen on the pad while looking over Sonntag's shoulder: An inventory clerk had clicked a knob on a stereo receiver confiscated as evidence. Nothing for a moment.

Then it began ticking. Clicking the knob back would not stop the sounds. The stereo receiver was presumed to contain a bomb.

Sonntag filled Ettinger in on the rest as the two grabbed their coats and went out the door of their office. The delivery boy arrived to an empty room. He shrugged, left the paper bag on top of a pockmarked steel worktable and went back to the restaurant.

The Kevlar suits were designed to protect them against the effects of premature detonation of up to three tons of force per square inch. But Sonntag and Ettinger knew that nothing could guarantee their safety against the range of explosive devices that it was possible to manufacture, even using off-the-shelf components. They stood in the cinderblock-walled room and looked at the problem.

"Well, Siggie, what have we here?" Ettinger opined, "a bomb maybe?"

"Could be, Fritzl," Sonntag replied. "At least it makes a ticking noise like a bomb, *jah*?"

The stereo receiver lay in the middle of a steel table that was bolted to the cement floor. It was clearly, though faintly, ticking, which meant that the bomb, whatever it was made of, was connected to a simple mechanical clock timer.

Sonntag and Ettinger pulled down the tempered Plexiglas face shields on their helmets and got to work. Throat mikes and armored videocams mounted on two corners of the walls recorded what they did and allowed other technicians in an adjoining room to feed back their comments.

"Have you ever wondered, Siggie," Ettinger said as he began to work on the screws holding the L-shaped top of the cabinet in place along the rear and sides of the receiver, "why anybody in their right minds would want to do our jobs?"

Hansl watched his partner intently as he unthreaded two, three, then four black carbide steel screws and laid them on the tabletop, then set down the screwdriver and prepared to lift up the top section.

"Nobody in their right minds would want to do this work," Sonntag answered. "This is obvious, jah?"

"I guess we should have our heads examined, eh Siggie?"

"You are right about that, Fritzl," replied Sonntag. "We are both certifiable lunatics."

"But we enjoy it, don't we?"

"*Jah*, but not as much as a good piece of ass," Siggie told Hansl. "We are not that crazy."

"Nobody is that crazy, Siggie," Fritzl answered with a laugh.

The banter stopped as the job started getting hairier. Not finding a motion sensor the bomb disposal experts determined that it was safe to open the case. Ettinger gingerly held the metal cover about a half inch above the base of the receiver unit.

The ticking was audibly louder now and the two cops could see colored wires that had no place in a stereo set around the edges. Sonntag already was in position with a fiber-optic probe attached to a video monitor, and he now moved the glowing tip of the probe along the interstices of the receiver.

The color video screen on the wall showed them a magnified view of the guts of the set. On it they could clearly discern the main components of the bomb.

They could see the main charge, a four-hundred-gram cylinder of rolled Semtex plastique. The Semtex had been covered with foil and festooned with a bar-coded label to make it look like a legitimate part of the set. Colored wires trailed beneath a nearby circuit board to an "ice cube" timing device linked to a chemical initiator, all of which bore phony bar-code labels like the Semtex. The components were connected to a travel alarm clock, hence the ticking, and a cluster of nine-volt batteries. It was a classic two-step bomb lashup. Once the clock timer closed an electrical circuit, a pulse of power would heat the ice-cube—actually a cube of solid incendiary component—which would combine with another chemical to initiate a thermite flash hot enough to detonate the Semtex.

Apart from this, they found nothing—such as a mercury tilt switch or other motion-sensing device—to indicate that the bomb was booby-trapped against tampering, apart from the on-off button that had been rigged to start the bomb ticking if depressed. Ettinger breathed a sigh of relief. He now lifted the top of the bomb completely clear of the base and set it down beside it on the worktable.

Suddenly the ticking stopped.

Ettinger and Sonntag had only a moment to look at each other before the near-pound of Semtex went off with a tremendous bang. In the enclosed space of the room, the force of the explosion was magnified as it bounced off the cinderblock walls and the reinforced concrete floor and ceiling, blowing the steel-plate blast door clean off its hinges and out into the hallway. The blast ripped the two cops limb from limb, flinging pieces of their bodies against the walls, ceiling and floor despite their protective clothing.

Only the bolted steel table remained in one piece, though its top, which had reflected the blast wave upward, now bore a deep bowl-shaped crater in its center.

The lorry was marked with the name and lightning bolt logo of Zeus, a Bonn firm specializing in overseas freight shipment. Arrangements for the truck to pick up a standard rectangular cargo container for airfreighting to Baghdad, Iraq, had been made the previous day.

The shipping firm had made all the arrangements and filed all the necessary paperwork, including the shipping manifests which stated that the eight-foot-square module contained agricultural equipment manufactured in Germany.

The company had sent two men out on the job, who now sat at either end of the truck, one in the cab listening to a news station on the radio, the other loitering at the rear, directly above the pneumatically actuated step-hoist that had been lowered to the ground, awaiting the appearance of the cargo container.

The shippers in the small brown-brick factory building had told them to wait until they had completed loading and sealing the container, which would require another few minutes. The two truckers were now doing just that. Waiting.

Inside the dark recesses behind the loading dock, Dr. Jubaird Dalkimoni sat inside the climate-controlled and specially padded freight container into which he had just lowered himself to the accompaniment of prayers for his safety and a swift journey to the sanctuary of his Arab brethren. The small factory was owned by an Iraqi agent-in-place; its staff had been dismissed early, and only trusted cadre remained behind. Dalkimoni's trip would not be all that long or that difficult, and it beat a stay in a Berlin jail cell any day of the week.

In minutes the bomb-maker saw hands lowering the airtight steel lid of the crate overhead and heard the thuds and snaps of heavy latches being pulled down and secured into place. Then, with a sudden lurch, he was picked up by a forklift and rolled out to the loading dock, where, with another series of juddering lurches the container was pneumatically hoisted to the level of the truck's floor, eased onto a pallet and wrestled inside by its crew.

Minutes later the terrorist heard the clank of the truck's rear doors slamming shut and the motor start up; the monotony of the ride to the airport was broken by the entertainment of the small color TV/video combo Dalkimoni been provided. The cargo container passed through customs without incident. Its waybill was in order and the shipping firm was an old and respected concern which transported hundreds of tons of freight per week in and out of Germany for its various clients.

In a matter of hours, Abu Jihad was heading south by southeast at four hundred fifty miles per hour, at a thirty-thousand-foot altitude, on a flight trajectory that would land him at Baghdad International Airport at eleven A.M., local time.

Once the plane landed, his glory and influence would be assured. The container would be commandeered by a special contingent from the Iraqi *Da'irat al Mukhabarat al Amah*, otherwise known as the Iraqi General Intelligence Service or GID, who reported directly to the office of Iraqi president Saddam Hussein. The GID would load the huge steel box on a military flatbed truck and whisk him to the agency's vast complex in Baghdad's Mansour district, nicknamed the "Great Wall of China" by knowl-edgeable locals.

There, in one of the many soundproof, surveillance-proof floors sunk below ground level, the module would be opened and Dalkimoni would be accorded a hero's welcome, which would culminate in the honor of a special audience with the president himself in his office at what had once been the U.S. Embassy in Baghdad.

Dalkimoni only had to endure the cramping of this en-closed space for a little while longer. He patted the spe-cially made vest he wore beneath his loose clothing, its six pouches containing as many hard cylindrical objects. Yes, he thought, these precious gifts would insure that his welcome would be as glorious as he surmised.

chapter *five*

Saxon studied the road in front of him from behind the wheel of the rented Mercedes sedan. The road he traveled was picturesque, winding its way through high Alpine meadows dotted with quaint cottages, steepled churches and apple orchards.

Beyond everything, shrouded in dense mists, loomed the snow-capped peaks of the Alps. Saxon knew they were mere foothills, called the Glarner Alpen by natives, that the true Alps began farther north. Then again, this was Tyrolean, Switzerland, and to the Tyrols a mountain was the Matterhorn; anything less was just a hill.

The road was more than a picturesque route through photogenic Swiss countryside, though. It was part of the body of a snake. The snake was long, with its fanged head in Germany and its rattled tail thousands of miles and half a world away in Pakistan.

The Bonn-Karachi truck route used this stretch of road through the high Alpine passes, just as it used dusty mountain roads in Afghanistan, and other roads in yet more remote places. Here, in the land of bread and chocolate, the snake's scales sparkled in the noonday sun. But there were other parts of the reptile far uglier to look at.

The snake was a survivor. Nothing could break its back. Not wars, not famines, not madness, not death. Down it went, through the chaos in the Balkans. Not even the fierce ethnic warfare that divided Croats from Serbs, Kosovars from Albanians, Slavs from Turks, that had drawn in the U.S. and NATO to police it, not even this could stop it.

On it passed, through Greece and into Turkey, and along the northern tiers of Syria and Iraq. Into Iran it weaved its serpentine track, and then down, down it slithered, all the way to its final destination, Pakistan.

Day in, day out, year in, year out, convoys of trucks passed along this trade artery between East and West. Only a global war might shut it down. Nothing less ever would. The truck route was too vital, too efficient, too useful to the many nations it serviced.

The overland route was easily a fifth as long as the comparable sea route—one that would need to cross the Mediterranean, pass down the length of the Suez Canal, come out into the Red Sea and then hook around into the Persian Gulf—and only a fraction of its cost. Nothing could match it. The truck corridor would be kept open, come what may. Too many global customers depended on it.

But the snake lived at a price. Refrigerators, televisions and stereos, fresh produce, new cars, and other domestic goods flowed along its back. Yet hidden beneath its underbelly was a far different type of traffic.

Here passed heroin and the opium base needed to manufacture the drug, and virtually any form of embargoed

goods. Along this same route Iraq was now receiving
components for its ongoing nuclear chemical and biological programs.

The snake was deadly. Its fangs dripped poison. But it
had many powerful friends, and no one would dare to
undermine it.

Until now.

Saxon turned the Mercedes off the road and swung the
silver luxury sedan onto a narrow dirt track that ran
straight across the meadow toward the small adzed-beam
cottage a quarter mile ahead. A few minutes later the car
had reached its destination.

Saxon parked on the gravel drive and the team emerged
from the Mercedes, the five men stretching their legs,
hauling luggage from the trunk and unfastening pairs of
skis from the rack at the top of the roof. To any observer
the men, dressed in *après-ski* gear, would have appeared
to be tourists out to catch the last *shusses* of the fast-
waning winter season.

Anyone interested in, and capable of, checking further
would learn that the group had come from Eastlake, Ohio,
a municipal subdivision of greater Cleveland, and that
they were all local real estators working for Century 21
on a week-long European ski junket.

The only discrepancy noted would have been a black
vinyl body bag that two of the men carried inside. The
body bag contained roughly a hundred pounds of aluminum beer cans and crushed ice. But it was a 1-Patcher
tradition to drink your hydraulic sandwiches out of a body
bag, and that was that.

The chalet, which was short-stay rental property leased
to visitors by a local landowner, had been paid for in

advance through a well-known travel agency. The Mercedes was also a rental, also booked in advance through an internationally reputed firm, which had also arranged for international drivers licenses for two members of the ski party.

That would have ended scrutiny of the five men, and so none would have been made suspicious by one of the five who, shortly after the other four had entered the chalet and drawn the blinds, stepped outside to have a smoke and admire the scenery.

Top kick Berlin' Hirsh did indeed admire the Alps, which reminded him of the Catskills in a funny way, except that none of the hotels served brisket of beef or prune juice. Hirsh also kept his eyes peeled for anybody on their way to the chalet while the team unpacked and checked the gear.

Saxon's checklist of weapons, explosives, timing devices, night vision goggles and other equipment had been precise and calculated down to the last battery and bullet.

With the blinds drawn, Saxon and the other members of the squad took everything out of the luggage in which an employee of the car rental company—a longtime CIA proprietary—had packed the stuff. It took the better part of an hour for all the gear to be checked out, put together, then broken down again and stowed away, but when it was finished Saxon was pleased to note that everything he'd ordered was there and ready.

For the greater part of the rest of the week, the team would play the role of dumb, drunk, horny, loud but good-natured and fun-loving Americans on vacation. Some of that would be real, since it would be a vacation from military life and the special warfare battlefield. Other parts of it would be the application of hard tactical lessons.

Their objective was the Deutsche Wehrteknik plant situated just outside the nearby ski town of Chur. By the end of the week the team would have secretly entered the factory and destroyed weapons components that DWT was thought to be manufacturing and secretly shipping to Iraq along the Bonn-Karachi truck pipeline.

Dr. Jubaird Dalkimoni relaxed in a Jacuzzi hot-tub with nubile whores catering to his every whim. The flat-screen HDTV was above the whirlpool bath, tuned to CNN. Dalkimoni fondled the large breasts and protuberant nipples of the blond Swedish girl while admiring the swaying ass on the black English girl who licked the blond's snatch while he watched TV.

The girls, the champagne, and the beautiful villa—it was as if he had awakened to a living dream of paradise promised in the Q'uran. It was rumored to have been the same villa in which Carlos had lived before his capture and imprisonment by French agents. Once a promising operator, and a rising star after his brilliant work at the Munich Olympics of 1972, he'd gotten too full of himself to remain effective. Besides, he was not an Arab. How could an infidel nonbeliever ever truly support the cause? Absurd.

Earlier, Dalkimoni had met with the presidential heir-apparent, Qusay Hussein, at the Old Presidential Palace in central Baghdad, across the Tigris River from the mixed commercial and residential Karada district. The palace was a complex of buildings off July Fourteenth Street between Ba'ath Party headquarters and the International Communications Center.

Qusay was in his fifth-floor office feeding his prize Siamese fighting fish, which he kept in a large tank that had been specially built into one of the office's imported hardwood walls—with the fabled cedars of Lebanon long gone, the wood for the walls had come from the Brazilian rainforest.

Qusay bred the fighting fish himself, and they had won him renown throughout the Middle East and the jet-set capitals of Europe. Qusay beckoned Dalkimoni to join him by the tank as he admired his finny warriors.

"It has been scientifically demonstrated that fighting fish grow balls when successful in warfare and lose them when disgraced or defeated," Qusay declaimed, staring into the tank and ignoring his visitor. "In defeat, the fish also shrink in size."

"This is most interesting, Excellency," replied Dalkimoni, standing at a respectful distance from his benefactor. "Most interesting, indeed."

Qusay continued to ignore the bomb-maker while he carefully sprinkled live, wriggling mealworms, beetle larvae and other small insects onto the surface of the water in the tank. Their struggling movements quickly attracted the predators below.

Qusay had a team of insect farmers in the basement on his payroll. The team did nothing except breed insects as food for Qusay's prize fish. At each morning's feeding, the choicest bugs were gathered by his breeders and delivered in a medium-sized jar to Qusay's office.

It was from this jar that Qusay was plucking tasty morsels with a pair of tweezers when the bomb-maker had come in.

"You see," Qusay went on, speaking toward the tank as if Dalkimoni were not even in his presence, "the defeated fish must either find a way to regain their balls or suffer annihilation. The only way for a fish to achieve this transformation is to fight. Thus, the fish are constantly at

war with each other. They live out their lives in a state
of perpetual combat."

Qusay had dropped another few wriggling bugs into the
tank, smiling as the fish jostled and pushed each other
aside, struggling to be the first to snap up the life-giving
morsels. The bomb-maker realized that Qusay was deliberately withholding most of the contents of the insect jar,
forcing the Siamese fish to crowd one another so that the
less aggressive ones would end up starving to death.

Finally, Qusay turned to face the bomb-maker. In his
eyes Dalkimoni saw the same strange fire that he had wit-
nessed in a rare interview with the *Rais*, or Iraqi leader,
Saddam Hussein. One day soon, Qusay would assume the
mantle of his father. Whether he would last very long was
an open question.

Unknown assailants had already voted against his stew-
ardship by attempting to shoot his car out from under him,
landing him in the hospital for months. Qusay, Dalkimoni
reflected, might well prove even more ruthless than Saddam; but he was far less popular and perhaps less cunning.
Still, time would tell the tale.

Screwing the cap back on the jar and laying the tweezers atop the lid, Qusay stepped away from the tank and
went to his cigar humidor. As if by magic, a lackey appeared and snipped the end off the cigar, lighting up his
master, and then vanishing into a side room.

Concentrating on his cigar and still completely failing
to acknowledge the presence of the bomb-maker by so
much as a single glance in his direction, Qusay issued his
last proclamations on the subject of Siamese fighting fish.

"There is a lesson here. An important one. We must
always fight and we must always prevail. We must never
tire, lest we should lose our balls. For if we should lose

our balls, we shall no longer be men, and then we shall inevitably lose our lives as well."

"You are truly wise, Excellency," the bomb-maker had then replied, and after a respectful pause, added, "Have you perchance reviewed the plan I presented?"

Qusay replied that he had, and that it had gained his approval.

"You may proceed," he told Dalkimoni, continuing not to look in his direction. But he added, "You have left out the traitor Farouk Al-Kaukji. The Rais himself has asked that something be done about this poisonous little toad."

"Don't worry about Farouk." Dalkimoni now spoke confidently, for he had already made ironclad arrangements to deal harshly with the traitor. "You may assure the *Rais* that he shall be taken care of quite soon."

"You meant immediately, did you not?" Qusay asked.

"Yes, Excellency. Of course. Immediately. Do not fear. It shall be done. Immediately."

"Good. I had not doubted this."

Qusay then left the office without uttering another word, leaving the bomb-maker standing by himself just inside the open door inhaling a sour cloud of secondhand cigar smoke.

Dalkimoni now understood that he was dismissed. He too left the building for his villa.

Back in Berlin, Farouk Al-Kaukji had been released by the German cops due to pressure from above. The federal government did not relish the dirt that a trial would dredge up.

Germany's notorious scandal sheets and tabloid television media would have had a field day—*Der Stern*, the government had learned, was already working on a cover story—and some of the displaced muck would certainly wind up covering a few powerful men in the Bundestag who had strong business and political ties to Baghdad. This could not be permitted to happen.

With charges against him dropped, Farouk Al-Kaukji disappeared immediately. He was spirited through various safe houses to Frankfurt, where another air-freight escape was being prepared by a surviving cell of the terrorist underground.

"Go with Allah," Farid Housek—who had been released on bail—bid him, hugging and kissing Al-Kaukji as he eased himself into a shipping container similar to the one in which his leader had fled Germany. "For those among the holy shall be blessed with everlasting grace."

Al-Kaukji kissed and hugged his cousin in return, then checked his oxygen supply and the seals on the pressurized interior lining and made sure that the freight module's interior light worked.

Everything seemed in order. The container might have been cramped, but he had been supplied with all the comforts of home for his journey. There was a pocket-sized edition of the *Quran*, plenty of snack food and canned soda, even some *Playboy*s and a bottle in which to take a leak when it became necessary.

There was also a roll of toilet paper, but he didn't see what it would be for, unless for wiping his dick if he got too carried away by the girlie magazine. Al-Kaukji tried to make himself as comfortable as possible. After all, for the next fifteen hours or so, this crate would be his home.

Two hours later, the crate was being forklift-loaded onto the baggage compartment of Sabena flight number 787, Frankfurt-Baghdad.

At the same time, a passenger named Sadoon Daher, a Cairo college student, bid so long to his new girlfriend,

Ulrike. She'd met him on the Ku'damm and had proven to be an expert in the Teutonic art of playing the blue-veined piccolo.

It had been an unforgettable two weeks of magic flute practice, with memories of Ulrike's flying ass and bouncing boobs enough to last him through many weeks of wanking material. Until he could find another blond girl with humungous lungs to play the flute with, that is. And Ulrike had given him a new boom box as a parting token of her affection.

The boom box went into Sadoon's luggage, and was placed only a few feet from where Al-Kaukji's freight container was located, with Al-Kaukji inside flipping through the *Playboy* as he ate sparingly, crumbs falling on the naked crotches of the blond twins that the caption said were from the American town of Modesto, California, home of locally produced wines of international distinction.

Sabena Airlines flight 787 was a direct flight whose route swung it steadily southward. The jet airliner's flight plan called for most of the journey to be made over water, crossing first the Adriatic and then the Mediterranean seas before transiting land again, hours later, as it passed over the littoral coast of Lebanon. The Alpine regions of Switzerland would mark the plane's last overflight of land for another five hours of travel time.

The flight passed over the Arlberg valleys at eight in the morning, at twenty-five thousand feet. It had reached its cruising altitude forty-five minutes before the lovely Ulrike's present did what the Iraqi cell that used her as a convenient gofer and frequent pump had programmed it to do.

A combination of flight time and altitude—this bomb had a dual timer/barometric blast initiator mechanism—

triggered the ice-cube fuse of the bomb which had been secreted in a sheet metal–sided cargo hamper in forward baggage compartment 14L, located just aft of the pilot's cabin and below the "S" in the Sabena logo.

Farouk Al-Kaukji was arguably the first casualty of the explosion, feeling the blast effects a third of a second before anyone else on the plane was incinerated. Altogether, it was a strange way to die.

Melting, shattering, exploding—all three at once. Without warning or preamble. Without absolution or transition. Dying in the flash of a moment, dead even as the realization of what was happening was making its way along nerve channels leading to the brain.

After that, he was nothing. No Allah, no Islamic paradise of *Behesht Zahra*, no ageless harlots to warm eternity awaited him. Unlike Sadoon Daher, Al-Kaukji didn't even have the most fleeting memory of Ulrike's winsome smile and nubile ass to speed him on his one-way trip to nowhere. The overtaxed and overstimulated neurons of Al-Kaukji's cerebral wetware were far too busy registering the panic at the death of his body for anything as complicated as that.

Far below, twenty-eight thousand feet below to be exact, it was ski season in the picturesque valleys, mountain passes and high meadows of the Glarner Alpen. On the snow-covered slopes around the trendy Swiss Alpine village of Chur, colorfully dressed skiers were startled by the sudden fireball in the skies and the thunder of multiple explosions that quickly followed the sighting.

For most the experience would begin and end there. For less fortunate others, it would have lasting consequences or be the cause of sudden death amid the festive atmosphere of a carefree ski holiday. As the plane broke apart in midair, jagged fragments of fuselage, gouts of flaming fuel and falling debris of every kind subjected the ski slopes to an unexpected aerial bombardment.

At least one skier had his limbs torn off by flying chunks of razor-edged steel, and several more had their brains bashed in by miscellaneous objects, including the decapitated head of one of the flight attendants, which crashed into the hapless skier it chanced to strike like a cannonball made of meat and bone.

In another case, an entire row of seats from the economy class cabin plunged through the roof of a ski chalet to crush two men and a woman engaged in three-way sex, flattening the trio and fusing their mashed corpses together, making it extremely difficult to separate them for autopsy later on.

For the next several weeks, morgue details were pulling arms, legs and various other assorted body parts out of the snow around Chur, and it would not be until spring came and the edelweiss again bloomed that the entire mess could be finally cleaned up and Chur returned to normal as a magnet for the international jet set and the globe-trotting rich.

A fter having had time to mull over his master's performance at the Old Presidential Palace earlier that day, the chief bomb-maker had absorbed the full meaning of Qusay's lecture about fish and balls.

The point was not lost on Dr. Jubaird Dalkimoni—he needed a success. Failure would not be tolerated.

The operation had been technically successful—the Columbine Heads had been assembled in Berlin from stolen Israeli weapons plans and brought intact to Baghdad. But the operation in Germany had needed to be closed down due to the carelessness of Dalkimoni's accomplices.

Nevertheless, Dalkimoni knew that Berlin remained the optimum place in Europe to assemble bombs. Much of the municipal police force was corrupt there, and the government had no stomach for risking the ire of rogue Arab states—there was far too much money invested both officially and privately, in defense and construction contracts with Middle Eastern despots. There were also plenty of ex-Nazis still alive and well in the Arab world, and they were powerful middlemen who had to be appeased as well.

For now, though, Berlin was too hot. It would still be months before operations could resume. But resume they would. Dr. Dalkimoni decided that if he wanted a place in the coming action, he had better not fuck up in his present assignment. But he would not. He was on the beam and would stay that way.

Suddenly Dalkimoni's attention snapped back to the present. The imported Swedish talent with a set of perfect 38D's was playing a stimulating pizzicato on his violin neck, getting him ready for a broadside across her tonsils. Right around when he thought he'd solo, the reporter on the TV cut away to CNN headquarters, where coverage of the breaking story of the bomb that had blown up a 747 jumbo jet over Switzerland was in progress.

Dalkimoni laughed out loud, something he always enjoyed doing while getting good head from a talented whore. He laughed now for a good reason: He had succeeded, and Farouk, the little *mahmoon* of a traitor, had paid in full measure for his cowardice and treachery.

The bomb-maker now also realized that Qusay had been absolutely correct concerning his little Aesop's fable too. He now understood that it was with men exactly as it was with Siamese fighting fish. This was completely true. Dr. Dalkimoni knew this for a certainty, for in the space of a split second, his balls had surely grown to twice their former size and girth.

Now he pulled the giggling girl's head underwater and felt her do what she did best. The bomb-maker orgasmed violently, pushing the Swede's head onto him as video footage of the fireball erupting over the Swiss Alps, caught by a tourist with a videocam, filled the large, flat-panel screen and holding the head there for quite a long time as the girl struggled for air, releasing her finally just before she went completely limp.

A mong those witnessing the fiery bolide in the Swiss skies were five men. Two of them were in a waiting Mercedes; the other three moved quickly and silently across the deserted grounds of the Deutsche Wehrteknik munitions plant.

The team had found what they were looking for at DWT. Within a secure, vaulted room of the plant, Saxon and two of the Marines had discovered a cache of Columbine Heads. These were rapid initiation devices, something like the Kryton switches for nuclear detonation secured by Saddam Hussein years before.

Columbine Heads were used for conventional explosives. But not just any kind of conventional explosives.

You needed Columbine Heads to trigger the ignition of air-dispersed effluents. You needed Columbine Heads, in short, for use with chemical, nuclear and biological agents or even fuel-air explosives.

Saxon and his team had left a calling card. The skull-and-crossbones Ace of Spades would be discovered later on by one of the guards, or before, if the one they'd tied up managed to free himself of the gag and handcuffs that now secured his arms and legs. Actually, they had left two calling cards—the first one and something else besides.

Saxon and the other two Marines hustled into the Mercedes, which gained the road from the nearby grove of fruit trees in which it was hidden, and drove off in the direction of Italy. The team would not be returning to the leased chalet, nor would the car be returned to the Swiss rental office. It would be picked up by someone else, on the other side of the Italian border near Ticino.

Behind them, a few minutes on the road, there was a sudden explosion. In just a little while, the local fire department had its hands full dealing with yet another five-alarm blaze in a morning that had been nothing short of a pyromaniac's dream. This particular one happened to have taken place at the Swiss headquarters of Deutsche Wehrteknik.

It apparently had nothing to do with the downing of Sabena flight 787, for the site of the explosion was far from any of the falling aircraft debris. Months would pass before the details were fully known, because at the moment the Swiss authorities had enough on their plate just sorting out the aftermath of the airline bombing.

In the meantime, Deutsche Wehrteknik would find itself facing some very disgruntled customers from Baghdad, causing the company president, Heinrich Alois Schmetterer, to leave for a protracted stay in the Canary Islands, where the sea breezes were said to be exceptionally healthful at that time of year. Certainly more healthful than facing a GID hit squad dispatched from the Old Presidential Palace.

But no one would ever figure out why a body bag full of melted ice and crushed beer cans was found abandoned in one of the chalets in a picturesque valley near the trendy jet-set ski town of Chur.

chapter *six*

Secretary of Defense Lyle Dalhousie sat in the rear of the black Lincoln Town Car that rolled along Pennsylvania Avenue through backed-up midmorning traffic and cold, relentless rain. Dalhousie's destination was the West Wing entrance of the White House, where the president and members of the National Security Council were awaiting his impending arrival.

To the SecDef's chagrin he realized that most of the morning was already gone and that it was approaching noon. Dalhousie had not eaten except for the vanilla ice cream sandwich he'd had for breakfast, bought at the Pick 'N Pay at the Pentagon Mall. Mountains of ice cream and seas of black coffee kept the Pentagon going; the Building thrived on caffeine and sugar. At least, Dalhousie knew, there would be sandwiches and soft drinks served at the White House.

Dalhousie did not find it at all strange to be preoccupied with his stomach in the midst of a regional war and a deepening international crisis, but this too went with the territory. As SecDef, he weathered whatever storms the Department of Defense weathered, and these were always legion.

The Building was like a ship in troubled waters, constantly buffeted by the gales of discord that blew in from the four corners of the globe. Keeping that ship trimmed to an even keel required a mental compartmentalization that kept things in perspective. Napoleon had likened this to opening one drawer of a filing cabinet while closing another, and Napoleon, Dalhousie reflected, was a commander who could go to sleep in the midst of a battlefield if he chose.

Dalhousie checked his watch and stared out the window, preparing himself for the approaching meeting at the NSC situation room in the White House basement beneath the Oval Office. He estimated another ten minutes, maximum, before he reached the West Wing gate. Meanwhile the SecDef's thoughts turned back to the events of the morning.

The early meeting in Dalhousie's third-floor E-ring office had been mandated by the events transmitted over the global SPINTCOM and CRITICOM (special and critical intelligence communications networks, respectively) the night before. Along these intelligence nerve channels had poured scattered reports throughout the previous day of Russian NBC weapons deployment in the Caucasus, but these reports had been disproved. Not so the reports of last night.

As the hours passed, the network of computers, fiber-optic cables and secure radio links that made up SPINTCOM/CRITICOM fed data from battlefield reports, spysat imaging and electronic intercepts to crisis management centers in the United States, including the Pentagon's

NMCC and the Emergency Command Center at the White House. These reports made the picture dismally clear. The Russians had almost certainly used chemical artillery strikes against Uzbeki rebels near the town of Igdir.

Unfortunately, this fact alone wasn't very surprising, only the potential of confirmation. Since the start of the Second Balkan War the previous year, after worsening tensions in Macedonia, the Russian army had swept into the Southern Caucasus and breakaway Azerbaijani republics in an attempt to stem the flood tide of ethnic rebellion that threatened to eat away at the flanks of the former Soviet empire.

The Soviet presence in Bulgaria had set Yugoslavia ablaze with war and tied up NATO and European Self-Defense Initiative forces in that regional theater. It had been deliberately calculated to divert the world's attention from the Soviet counterinsurgency campaign on Russia's southern flank. As a diversion, Moscow Center's strategy had been fairly successful, though otherwise it had proved a dismal failure.

Instead of destroying separatist guerilla enclaves, the campaign had merely broken them up and dispersed the survivors to found new fighting cells. Ethnic rebellion had spread rather than waned, driving separatist exiles into border enclaves in northern Iraq, southern Turkey and northern Iran, where they formed liaisons with Peshmerga—Kurdish rebel forces—scattered in these areas. Ethnic unrest was now spreading into the Middle East and toward the flanks of NATO, and this latest news from the front showed that the Russians were in desperate straits.

The Soviet debacle had been the subject of the breakfast meeting in the SecDef's office, attended by the chiefs of staff, the CJCS, the DepSecDef, and other deputies and assistants.

Dalhousie had sat at his customary place behind the enormous Pershing desk that had bolstered the dignity—and more often the feet—of his predecessors at the post, and while his secretary served fresh coffee and a polite young Marine officer wheeled in a tray of bagels, danishes and muffins, Dalhousie had begun the discussion about strategies, options and political damage control.

CJCS Starkweather had as usual argued for his pet project, the Snake Handlers. But "Bucky's SMF's," as they had come to be called by the chairman's critics at the Building, had temporarily gone inactive. The special missions unit led by Ice Trencrom had caused a crisis in the Pacific the previous month on a mission to stem China's acquisition of silent Kilo-class submarines equipped with cruise missile delivery technology. The subs no longer posed a problem, but the destruction of a multibillion-dollar sub pen complex off the coast of Kinmen Island had created political fallout that the president was still ducking.

Trencrom's crew was not an option this time, thought the SecDef. But there were other hole cards that the U.S. might yet pull out of its sleeve. These would be discussed at the White House with the president and members of the NSC. Later that afternoon, after Dalhousie returned to the Building, there would be further discussions with the assembled chiefs in the Tank.

First things first, though. Just ahead, out of the late morning fog, loomed the black iron gate of the West Wing entrance. The Lincoln slowed, the gate was opened for the vehicle flying the DOD chief's flag, and the big limousine rolled inside, onto the White House grounds.

*   *   *

The National Security Council Situation Room is a small, soundproof meeting chamber buried two stories beneath—but not behind, as some claim, confusing it with the Cabinet Room—the president's Oval Office. The Situation Room is flanked by an operational command center staffed by military personnel which has available secure Hammer Rick communications links—commonly known as the "hotline"—direct to the Kremlin in Moscow.

The NSC Situation Room, which was constructed following the establishment of the National Security Act of 1947, which, among other things, created the CIA, has played host to numerous meetings prompted by international crises.

It is a cramped chamber dominated by a large square meeting table and lit by overhead light panels. The sit room is not a place conducive to comfort. It is a place of decision, a seat of judgment, and it looks and feels the part.

As the Secretary of Defense was ushered through the West Wing entrance of the White House, the NSC chamber was occupied, as it had been on many a crisis before, during and after the Cold War, though not by the president or his chief advisors.

A group of mid-level cabinet deputies manned the situation room this morning, providing a skeleton staff in the event of a new emergency. President Travis Claymore preferred to meet with advisors in the Oval Office whenever possible; the sit room made him claustrophobic.

Today was no exception, and the SecDef was informed upon arrival at the White House that the meeting was to be held in the Oval Office. A Marine guard soon ushered him into the famous circular room, where he found the small circle of the president's closest advisors already seated in the customary horseshoe arrangement of chairs just in front of the fireplace. The seating arrangement placed all advisors in positions facing the president's desk.

"Lyle, come in," said President Claymore. "We've been expecting you. Sit down. Help yourself to coffee. The turkey sandwiches are pretty good today."

Dalhousie took a BLT off the buffet that had been set up by the entrance and sat in a vacant seat, his customary one beside State near the center. The SecDef bit into the sandwich as the president leaned back in his desk chair and steepled his palms for a moment. Damn, he was hungry.

"Lyle, you know the shit that's been mellowing in the Caucasus. As of this hour we've got a hopper full of confirmed reports the Russians have used chemical weapons on the Uzbeks. I've already taken calls from the Europeans . . . President Le Blanc, Prime Minister Benchley, and several other heads of state have phoned to express grave concerns.

"I'm concerned about the possibility of the ESDI going off on its own hook and doing something dumb. In fact Margaret Thatcher was on the line just before you arrived. As you know she's been a strong opponent of the ESDI right from the start. She gave me a few ideas and I've enlisted her to take the pulse of the European military and political establishment on this issue."

"She's a grand lady, and a damn good ally to have in our corner, Travis," replied the SecDef after swallowing a bite of the sandwich. "If anybody can reign in the hawks in the ESDI—and I can think of two offhand—"

"Caillou and Potenza," interjected Russ Conejo, the White House national security advisor.

"And let's not forget our friend 'Falcon' Hull," put in Dougless Galvin, the secretary of state, technically outranking the SecDef but more often requiring the coordination of the national security advisor between the two major foreign policy departments. "That son of a bitch's been spoiling for a fight ever since the damn Gulf."

"All three. Certainly," agreed the SecDef, sandwich now finished. "Field Marshall Hull especially. Schwarzkopf threatened to punch him out to stop him from making a unilateral move on Baghdad."

That remark brought a laugh. Someone remarked, "It would have been a hell of a bout, though. In this corner, the Bear. In this corner, the Falcon."

"You were there, weren't you, Lyle?" chimed in State, after a fresh round of laughter.

"Damn right I was, Mike," answered Dalhousie. "And didn't Hull raise a stink over it too. If we hadn't kept as close a lid on the fucking press as we did back then, who knows what would have happened. It could have blown the "special relationship" right out of the water. And mind you, Hull was only a chickenshit two-star then. Today he's a field marshal."

"Gentlemen," the president interjected, silencing the byplay, "all this notwithstanding, we've gotta craft a policy on this issue. When this is over it's my intention to phone Premier Starchinov and address the issues directly. I want to be prepared." The president leaned forward. "Lyle, your assessment, please."

"Mr. President," replied the SecDef, "this morning I conferred with the Chiefs of Staff. As you know, we have been monitoring the situation closely. We are gravely concerned about the implications of this action on the part of the Soviets, but more along the lines of ancillary or corollary actions that might flow from it than the action itself."

"Explain."

"Mr. President, as Burt may have already told you (he referred here to Burlington Downes, Director of CIA), while we have confirmed the Soviets' deployment of a chemical weapon—delivered by long-range artillery—all evidence so far points to the agent's being a fairly benign, if I may use that word, form of antipersonnel agent."

"We'd discussed the agent, CS-X, with the president just before you arrived, Lyle," added the CIA director, addressing Dalhousie.

"OK. Then Travis, you already know that what we're dealing with here's essentially a very concentrated form of tear gas, which in military strength can cause severe vomiting, dizziness and shortness of breath."

"Yep, I heard that, Lyle," answered Travis from behind the presidential desk. "But CS-X is also like a nerve gas in some ways, isn't it, and can be lethal."

"Travis, Mr. President, yes, yes it can," replied the SecDef. "That's true. I don't want to give you the false impression that it's not a powerful or potentially deadly weapon they used. But I want to put it into perspective. Compared to chemical agents we know the Soviets to have available to them—"

"The binary shells?"

"Yes, Mr. President, the binary weapons, or binary artillery shells if you will, these binary weapons can disperse truly horrendous nerve agents such as tabun or sarin, which are many orders of magnitude deadlier than those which the Soviets have used. They also have stocks of biologicals including anthrax and chimeric botulin available. Truly deadly, horribly deadly, agents."

"You said this word . . . ?"

"Chimeric?"

"Right."

"That means, Mr. President, that the viral or biological agent is an artificially mutated strain."

The president leaned back, silent a moment.

"Bucky wanted to turn loose those lunatic Snake Eaters on this Vector place out near Sebastopol somewhere. That's where all this germ shit they got's supposed to come from. What do you think of that?"

"Snake Handlers," the Secretary of State corrected.

"Right, Bucky's Snake Handlers."

"Mr. President, I have just a short while ago conferred with Chairman Starkweather and I can report that he and the chiefs of staff firmly agree that a strike on the Vector, or any other Soviet installation of its kind, would be neither strategically sound nor politically expedient at this time."

"Then what?"

"We believe that the use of CS-X agent was due to the indiscretion of a particular field commander acting under the authority of the FSB. As you know, the Kremlin has been frustrated by lack of progress against rebel forces. Control of many sectors has been taken from the GRU and placed in the hands of the state intelligence service, the FSB. The field commander in question is believed to have been recalled to Moscow.

"What concerns us is the threat of command and control slipping from Soviet military forces in theater, leading to the use of deadlier weapons of mass destruction farther down the line. Secondly, we're worried about the ESDI overreacting and doing something foolish. Thirdly, we're gravely concerned about the escalation of the Caucasus fighting to the fringes of neighboring countries, and fourthly—"

Suddenly there was a knock and the door of the Oval Office was opened by a Marine guard.

"Sorry I'm late," the CJCS said as he came in, accompanied by an aide carrying an assortment of maps, charts and audiovisual aids. "There was a really bad accident on the way. We got stuck in traffic."

"That's OK, Buck," said the president. "Have a seat. We'll fill you in. Lyle?"

"Actually, Mr. President," said Lyle Dalhousie, "the chairman's got all the presentation materials to fill you and the working group in on the fourth point I was about to get to. I think we should let him have the floor."

"Buck, how about it?" the president asked.

"Be happy to, Mr. President," replied the CJCS, and stepped to the fireplace, where his aide was already setting things up.

The premier of the neo-Soviet Communist government replaced the telephone receiver in its cradle and sat for a few moments gazing out the window of his dacha, across the grand, sloping greensward that ran parallel to the Moskva River for almost half a kilometer before the view was obscured by the beech woods surrounding the country estate.

The dacha was situated only a few miles from Moscow Center, yet was blessed with all the peace and solitude a man could want. A short ride from his Kremlin office, there was this solitude, and the general secretary took advantage of this fact whenever possible. Boris Andreyevich Starchinov now watched a freight vessel pass along the darkened river, its running lights revealing the ship's ghostly outline against the deeper darkness of night.

The general secretary's mind flashed back to his first encounter with the dacha, during the height of the August Revolution of 1991. What heady days they had been! As a young KGB agent, loyal to Kryuchkov, the director, he had been among those who had been handpicked to detain the traitor Gorbachev and his foulmouthed wife, Raisa, under house arrest.

Had he been given instructions to carry out the execution of the two traitors to the Party, Starchinov would have done so with pleasure. But the order had never come. Instead, there had been the ignominy of defeat and the ascendancy of the doddering *bizhdenok* Yeltsin and his *vlasti*—Oligarchs—to power at the Center. That had been the beginning of the end, though only for a time.

Little had Starchinov dreamt on that day, when both the birthmarked one and Raisa were in his grasp, that he would one day occupy this place some years later. He could thank the squint-eyed ferret Putin for the honor.

The fool had preferred him and all the while Starchinov worked against him. Of course, this is precisely what Putin's own sponsor, Boris Yeltsin, had done with Stepashin, Putin's chief rival, promoting the *poputchik* to fill the spot for which he was actually grooming the ferret. If nothing else, Yeltsin had been a master second only to Stalin in the fine art of using *poputchiks* to do his dirty work.

After disposing of Putin, Starchinov had hunted down Gorbachev and had him executed. In Red Square, the people had cheered. Putin had been his first *poputchik*. There had been several others since then. Tomorrow, there would be yet more. Such was the equation of power that it demanded *poputchiks* at every stage.

Boris Starchinov turned from the window, the ghost ship having disappeared into the gloaming. The eternal Moskva was again silent, the night still, and broken only by the chirping of crickets in the grass and trees. The Soviet premier and general secretary of the Party turned to his assembled advisors.

"I have considered the words of the U.S. president," he told them. "We have larger goals, and this incident must not be allowed to interfere."

"But the *chernozhopyi* rebellion. It must be crushed. And quickly. We are running out of time. This has turned into a real *bl'adki*." Some raised their eyebrows at the speaker's boldness in his choice of metaphors.

"Yes, it surely has become a circle jerk, Misha, I know this. And besides we seem always to be running out of time," Starchinov replied with sangfroid. Yet his lenslike eyes stared out, assessing the faces of his advisors, one by one, taking their measure in his gaze as it slowly passed across their faces.

Starchinov stood and snapped his fingers, a signal for his personal valet to hand him a vodka martini, his favorite drink. He sipped the alcohol and set the glass down on the desk.

Again his gaze crossed the faces of his advisors.

"*Tovarischi*—Comrades," he began. "Here is what I propose."

He began to tell them his plan, leaving out the fact that he had decided upon whom his next *poputchik* would be. When he would finish, the advisors would be asked their opinions.

No matter what their true thoughts, each would strive to outdo the other in voicing their wholehearted approval.

Twenty-five miles north of Tel Aviv, an unmarked limo with bulletproof glass, and tires capable of rolling at high speed even if struck by grenade shrapnel, nimbly ascended a steep, winding road. Its destination was a series of low-rise whitewashed buildings strung along the crest of a low bluff.

The complex, which included an Olympic-sized swimming pool, could easily had been confused with any number of resort hotels throughout Israel. The concealed snipers who monitored the limo's ascent up the serpentine drive suggested strongly that it was anything but that. In fact, the complex was the main—though not the sole—headquarters of the Israeli intelligence agency, Mossad.

The vehicle was expected. The concealed surveillance/sniper teams had been officially told only that it contained a VIP. However, the teams were familiar with the prime minister's personal car by this time and knew that Gershon Simchoni was paying a visit to the head of Mossad, former general Yehuda Peretz.

No one besides Simchoni, Peretz and a handful of close advisors knew the reason for the meeting, but those in the know had not slept well because of the knowledge they possessed.

Once again, Israel's existence was threatened by the Arabs surrounding it. Israel would have to launch defensive plan *Ken Tsa'rot*—"Nest of Hornets." The operation might well prove to be the most desperate one in that nation's history.

Ken Tsa'rot would have to work the first time. There would be no second chance. But then, Peretz mused, since when had it ever been otherwise for the Holy Land?

book two

*Special Weapons
and Tactics*

chapter *seven*

Insertion into the *Reshteh-ye Kuhha-ye Alborz*—the El-burz mountain range—had been a predictable bitch. A-Detachment of Marine Force One was on a tight timetable, and this added to the logistical problems faced by the 1-Patchers. Precision timing was vital to the successful outcome of One's mission. So was secrecy.

The 1-Patchers' presence in the Elburz would not evade the attention of Iranian Pasdaran or Iraqi *Sai'qa*—special security forces—for long, but the longer the presence of American "advisors" to rebel forces remained covert the better the chances for success.

Saxon and a company-strength element of One personnel had been in-country for approximately a month, training guerilla cadres in low-intensity warfare techniques. The guerilla groups were based in hidden encampments amid the many miles of barren, windswept hills making up the cross-border area between Turkey, Iran and Iraq, north of the twenty-fifth parallel.

Ethnic Kurds and Georgians from the bombed cities in the Caucasus made up the majority of these rebel fighting cells. The two main groups did not mix very much, except at the leadership levels, and occupied separate enclaves throughout the hill country. The groups had little in common politically or culturally, and although Islam was a shared religion for many of them, it was by no means the only religion they practiced.

Ethnicity and place of origin mattered much more to how the groups got along, and here the differences were often much greater than the similarities. The Georgians considered the Kurds "Turks," the Kurds considered the Georgians "Slavs." There was no doubt that had it not been for the common enemies confronting the both of them in the Moscow-Baghdad axis, they would have been at each other's throats.

And what were American commando advisors to them? Saxon had entertained no illusions about that from the first, nor, for that matter, about the true nature of his mission. Marine Force One had been reluctantly accepted because an American presence meant a source of arms, money, food and medicine.

The rebels cared not a whit for any training or expertise that might be part of the package. By now they had been waging their guerilla wars with their respective opponents for a very long time. Outsiders were not welcome. Nor could they ever be trusted. They might be used for a time, and then thrown to the mountain wolves, but never accepted, never brought into the community of *mostazafin*— the disinherited.

Saxon understood that attitude, and never tried to get chummy with the indigenous forces he and his men were training in these cold, arid mountains. That was always a mistake, as it had been in Southeast Asia and Afghanistan for U.S. spooks, military advisors and other even more questionable personnel carrying out stranger missions. It would have been even more of a mistake here because nobody was conning anybody anymore.

The political games had been played out in the Third World during the twentieth century and they no longer worked. Those who "went native" would be sucked dry and thrown away. Kurtzes would never be a match for the Heart of Darkness here. Indigenous guerilla forces viewed the U.S. as a fair-weather friend who would desert them as soon as the going got too tough. Nothing could shake that conviction because it had been proven correct far too many times.

It was now almost midway into the 21st century's first decade and alliances between the U.S. and guerilla forces were based on mutual need and greed—never trust. America wanted something from them; they wanted something from America. A deal would be done, and that was all there was to it. Anything else was merely a public relations sham to preserve a semblance of something deeper, but nobody believed it otherwise.

Saxon's team might have been conducting training exercises in the hills, but its true purpose was to carry out a strategic reconnaissance of the area. It was believed by the CIA that borderlands of the Elburz were being used as a secret conduit for weapons and embargoed weapons manufacturing materials.

The Soviets were ferrying in the stuff in a very risky manner. The Mean One's job was to take advantage of the opportunity to fuck them up.

Rempt inhaled deeply. Taking the last drag on the Russian nonfilter cigarette for all it was worth, he flicked the butt into the stiff wind blowing off the nearby ridge line. The spook exhaled the thick gray smoke through his nostrils and spat onto the dusty ground. He turned to Saxon.

"Let's go, partner," he said.

Saxon stared at Rempt. He did not like the spook, and trust was a term that had no meaning with respect to any intelligence personnel Saxon had ever encountered. Rempt was the CIA liaison with indigenous forces in the region.

A career Arabist, he had been shuttling around across the length and breadth of the Middle East for nearly three decades, much as Kim Philby had done in a previous era. Virtually all belonging to Rempt's type had a Lawrence of Arabia complex, and Rempt was no exception.

He spoke all the major languages and dialects of the region fairly fluently. When in the field, Rempt sported a *kaffiyeh* and burnoose and carried a short-barreled AKS autorifle slung over his shoulder and a dagger in his belt.

Saxon nodded his assent but said nothing else. He was ready. The small group of Kurdish rebels—the Peshmerga or "Fellows in Arms"—and 1-Patcher commandos occupied four-wheel-drive vehicles that though battered were as able along the rutted narrow mountain roads as pack mules. The reconnaissance team would be led by Rempt, who would also act as translator and mission coordinator.

Saxon had no intention of letting the spooks "coordinate" his mission beyond a certain point, however, and he knew full well that, in the field, Rempt's claim was tenuous. In the first place, General Patient K., Marine Force One's commander, would see to it that the Marine commandant spoke the necessary benedictions to the chairman of the Joint Chiefs.

In the second place, if Rempt started getting too bossy,

Saxon would simply frag the fucker. He would then report the unfortunate demise of CIA field agent Rempt in an enemy ambush. It would then be with Saxon like it had been with Major Strasser in the film *Casablanca*—a question of whether Rempt had either "hung himself" or was "shot trying to escape."

The windswept ridge was chosen as the ideal surveillance point for the main force element. The rest of the detachment was strung out along the ridgeline on a roughly two-mile front. The 4WD vehicles had been parked in natural hiding places and covered with camouflage netting, sand and rocky debris to shield them from aerial surveillance.

The hide sites would not have to hold up to scrutiny for very long. The mission would last little more than a few hours. It would be the waiting—against darkness and cold, fighting off fatigue in the monotony of these desolate hills, until the moment to act arrived—that would be the hardest part.

They would have to be fully alert then, for those few minutes. After that the opportunity window would shut tight, and what they had come to do might be impossible the next time around. The shoulder-fired antiaircraft missiles ported by the combined teams were for defensive purposes, and only to be used as a last resort. This was a recon mission, not an assault.

Far away from that lonely, desolate hill country in the Elburz, a Soviet advisor named Major Lavrenti Ogarkov scanned another distant horizon as he smoked a French Sobranie cigarette, which he preferred to native

Russian brands. He then looked toward his men, who he had permitted to fall out around the nearby circle of two-and-a-half-ton trucks near the desolate landing strip.

The Spetsnaz troops were well trained and expertly drilled. Even at ease, they looked precisely like what they were—soldiers, and superb ones too. Curse the *mudozhovaniki*, the shit-mouths, back at headquarters for wasting such soldiers as mere truck loaders, Ogarkov thought.

The Spetsnaz commander idly consulted his wristwatch. Time yet. Plenty of time to go until the expected cargo plane arrived. Again, he turned his attention to the desert barrens surrounding him.

The sere wasteland looked out across the Syrian Desert and into Saudi Arabia. Beyond was Jordan, then Israel and the Med. In time, war would break out here, and the Soviet Union would be in it for keeps.

The major continued to smoke. There was an iron logic to it all, but moreover, an iron inevitability. Ogarkov waited and watched, imagining a string of Soviet victories from the Persian Gulf clear to the Med, and the glory to be won in the coming fight.

At a little past 0400 hours they came. The stillness of the desert and hills had been broken only by the keening of the wind and the distant baying of jackals, wolves and other night predators. Now another sound began to creep into the night.

A man-made sound.

The sound began as a low rumble originating at a point far to the northeast. Soon it began to swell and surge. There was no mistake. The planes were coming.

Not that there had been doubt from the first. The team was not relying merely on its eyes and ears to sense the approach of its quarry. An array of compact battlefield computing and electronics equipment handled that part of the job.

High overhead, invisible to the naked eye, parked in a geosynchronous low earth orbit, an Improved Crystal Kennan–class photoimaging satellite kept its sensor array trained on a swath of territory on the earth below.

The Kennan—also known as Keyhole, KH, Big Bird and some other names besides its true, real and deeply classified name—had been jockeyed out of another orbit over another part of the world for use as an overhead surveillance asset dedicated to the mission.

Via a secure microwave downlink, the twelve-ton, fifty-five-foot-long spy satellite transmitted realtime photo-imaging to the team's mobile command center on the ground and, via crosslink to a TDRSS Infosat, to the NSA's sprawling Ft. Belvoir, Virginia, antenna farm; underground fiber-optic cables sealed in krypton gas-filled tubes and wired into pressure sensors against unauthorized interception, carried the feed from there to other cleared recipients, such as the CIA.

Saxon had been watching the planes for some time, seeing the well-coordinated aerial circus act by which the Russians were facilitating their convoy over hostile air-space. On the Washington Beltway, they called it "flying the Elburz Bottleneck," the most direct route from the large military transshipment depot at Kharkov, about three hundred miles due south of Moscow, to various offloading points in Iraq.

Direct yes, but only in terms of it being the shortest distance between two points. In every other respect, the route was extremely risky, requiring an overflight of approximately eight miles of Iranian borderland in the El-burz mountain chain—the so-called bottleneck.

Risky but still attractive. All other routes into Iraq were indirect sea routes requiring weeks to negotiate by freighter. The Russians had been tempted by the ease and speed promised by daring the bottleneck. They had decided to take their chances.

One thing that had encouraged the Russians was a six-mile gap in Iranian ground surveillance radar that their ferret aircraft had pinpointed during reconnaissance missions to study the feasibility of a military airlift into Iraq. The Chinese-made End Tray and Ball Point radars that the Iranians used were fixed stations that overlapped fairly well across most of the border, affording reliable coverage. Here they didn't.

With the aid of Tupelov TU-126 electronic intelligence (ELINT) aircraft to confuse Iranian radars farther north and south, and able pilots for the big Antonov AN-72 "Coaler" transports that were used to ferry in the loads, the plan was deemed workable. To provide further insurance, the Antonovs used regularly scheduled commercial Aeroflot shuttle flights between Moscow and Baghdad as additional cover against radar detection.

The military planes would coincide their takeoffs with an early morning Aeroflot commercial run, flying close against the commercial jetliner across Iranian territory. Once inside Iraq, however, the Antonovs would break free and continue on to their destinations. For added security, transponders identified the rogue military planes as commercial cargo aircraft, conforming to bogus flight plans.

The Russians had worked on the technique ever since the Americans had used it against them during the Reagan years, timing military surveillance overflights of Soviet North Pacific bases with scheduled passenger flights between Anchorage, Alaska and Seoul, Korea.

This particular run tonight followed the usual pattern.

A few miles shy of the Iranian border, over southern Azerbaijan, the Antonov Coaler heavy-lifter slipped into the flight path of Aeroflot flight 889 out of Moscow and bound for Baghdad International Airport. Farther to the southwest, a TU-126 "Moss" electronic countermeasures aircraft waited to conduct covert electronic warfare operations against the Iranian early warning radar fence.

As the two planes approached the border, the TU-126 turned on its active jamming. The Aeroflot flight slipped through the Iranian radar screen, with its military shadow plane undetected. The TU-126 monitored the passage for a while, keeping the corridor open for other Soviet air assets, then lumbered off to its base in Kharkov, its work done. As had been the case on the several other shuttle overflights, the Antonov then disengaged from beneath the Aeroflot passenger aircraft once it had passed the border.

The Antonov could now navigate on its own without much risk of detection, for here the mountains turned into a maze of great rifts bordered by steep, craggy massifs. Many of these high mountain passes were large enough for even an Antonov transport to navigate safely—if the pilot was alert, and skillful, and had luck on his side.

The Soviet air force had no difficulty finding pilots eager to accept the challenge, especially since the trip, though hazardous, was relatively short. The rift valleys only amounted to under fifteen minutes of total flight time. Once out of the maze, it was straight and easy going across the flat, unbroken reaches of the vast Iraqi desert. The way home was a safe, though longer route west, then north—the hazards existed on the inbound flight only.

So it was with this air resupply mission. Albeit with one important exception that the Russians did not know anything about.

*   *   *

Saxon knew all about it, though. And it had been what he had come to this desolate and forbidding mountain country to witness.

In only a few minutes Saxon and Rempt, who stood with their eyes alternately scanning the skies and fixed on the flat-panel screen of a portable battlefield computer, would be certain whether the prize was within their reach or not.

The minutes ticked off. The computer screen remained blank; the digital portal to another world stayed dark, empty. Saxon again turned his gaze to the skies. He no longer needed the light-amplifying gear to detect the arriving aircraft.

Though flying without lights, the Antonov was cruising less than twenty feet below the tops of the ridges flanking the high rift valley within which the surveillance team had taken shelter. There was enough ambient light to see the airframe limned darkly against the flanks of the towering bluffs.

Saxon admired the skill of the Russian pilot. It was an impressive feat of precision flying. He would have liked to watch the planes just soar through the chasm like immense pterodactyls, but the tactical computer's screen had come to life, and something more important had appeared, riveting his attention.

On the screen, the interior of the same Antonov that was now passing overhead was limned in shades of green and black. A procession of faces belonging to the contingent of soldiers onboard the aircraft seemed to move relative to the motion of the hidden camera onboard. Rempt was nodding his head.

"Beautiful," he muttered. "Fucking beautiful."

Saxon watched his face, transfixed with a perverse fascination.

"Absolutely fucking beautiful."

Rempt sickened him, especially since Saxon knew the source of the spook's glee. Onboard the Antonov was a surgically altered human, a cyborg. The man's name was Yevgeny Karlovich, and he had been forced to undergo a risky operation to graft sensing equipment onto his optic nerves.

Karlovich had been compromised in a monkey trap set by the CIA in Moscow and given a choice between a life sentence at the notorious Lubyanka prison or submission to the surgical procedure.

The nuclear physicist had developed a sex and drug habit that had been used to compromise him by field assets in Moscow. Nanotechnology had created a microminiature low-light camera and transmitter that could run by electrical impulses generated by the mitochondria of the optic nerve cells. It had been implanted in Karlovich's skull, in the cavity called the stylo-mastoid foramen, directly behind the eyes.

From that moment on Karlovich became the CIA's walking camera lens. He had been used extensively, and this was to be his final mission before deactivation. Karlovich had been promised asylum in Arizona and enough money to start his own insurance business under a new identity.

Far below, Saxon continued to watch, nauseated as much by this surgically altered monstrosity passing overhead, as by the unholy glee that Rempt exuded from every pore as he drank it in. Karlovich was following orders, feigning airsickness in order to be permitted to wander along the cabin for a while, transmitting back imagery of the plane's cargo in the process.

Now the physicist had reached the main cargo section. Clearly visible on pallets were tubular components in protective wooden casings, lashed securely with tie-downs to bolts on the aircraft's deck. There were large military transport cases as well, many of these bearing the universal warning symbol for radioactive materials.

"Shit, look at that," Rempt declared. "There's no doubt about what the Sovs are flying in now. No doubt."

The downlink of imagery continued as the airframe transited the Elburz. But the transmission was brief. The plane soon navigated the rift valley and vanished into the dark, across the border into Iraq. Moments later the silence of the night again descended across the isolated mountain barrens on the edge of nowhere.

"Let's—"

Rempt stopped in mid-sentence.

Something else was coming, something that hadn't been anticipated. Rempt quickly punched keys at the console of the mobile command station and let out a whistle. Saxon saw it there too, moments before they arrived— Mi-24 Hinds, two of them. Both mammoth gunship helicopters were heavily armed with rockets and automatic cannons.

Saxon judged they had been sent along on this mission to ride shotgun on an especially important cargo. Maybe the brass back at Kharkov had gotten nervous and wanted to add a little insurance coverage to the package. Whatever the reason, the Hinds had tagged along.

Suddenly Saxon saw the signs of struggle out of the corner of his eye. It was at a nearby rock ledge occupied by a group of Peshmerga. To his horror Saxon saw two men wrestling each other, heard their quarrelsome oaths echoing across the canyon, saw and heard other Peshmerga rushing to the scene.

Again he looked up toward the Hinds, relieved to see that they continued on along a straight path, for the moment oblivious to the commotion below.

Saxon turned his attention back toward the struggle. Now one of the Kurds knocked the other down and rose to his knees, and the dark silhouette of a blunt-ended tubular object described a tangent in the night as it pointed at the sky.

Damn—he was going to fire a Stinger missile at one of the Hinds.

Saxon moved quickly, sprinting across broken ground, his combat knife already unscabbarded, knowing what would have to be done, and done quickly, to avoid blowing the entire mission. As he advanced, Saxon saw the prone man rise and knock the other down before he could fire. The black tubular weapon fell into darkness once more. Saxon would not give it a second chance to sweep upward again.

In moments he had reached the scene of the continuing struggle. The first man had again shoved the other one down. Saxon approached the Kurd with the Stinger shoulder-fire weapon as he raised it again.

Saxon sprang and grabbed the hill man by the hair, pulling his head back and twisting his neck with a savage wrench. The neck broke in a second with a dull, wishbone-snapping sound and the man went limp. Saxon cradled the dying man's head in the crook of his arm, slowly lowering him to the broken earth and silencing any noises he might have made as life left him.

He lay prone and watchful beside the corpse, searching for the Hinds. To his chagrin he saw that the gunships had slowed their forward progress. They were now hovering in a search pattern, as though they had seen something on the floor of the ravine.

Saxon's hand moved to the missile launcher that had fallen near the dead man. If they attacked, he would have to use it anyway. There would be no other choice. The entire operation would be compromised and 1-Patcher commandos would probably be killed in the firefight that would follow.

In the air, the immense steel dragonflies darted and hovered, moved to and fro, circling through the canyons. Amplified by reflection off the sheer rock walls of the defile, the chugging of the Hinds' main rotors took on a deafening cadence, crept into the skull like rats into a hole, chewed its way into the brain.

It quickly became a contest of nerve, a battle against the fear-fed urge to strike first, before the Hinds shot up the valley with cannon fire or air-to-ground missiles, and the voice of prudent caution that counseled, "Stay put, wait it out, see what happens."

The Hinds continued to dart and hover, circle and dance, rise and fall. More tense moments ticked away. And then suddenly the two helos climbed for altitude and sped westward along the track of the departed Antonov.

Moments later they were gone.

Saxon was rolling the corpse of the Peshmerga guerilla who had been panicked into nearly firing at the Hinds into a convenient chimney in the rocks. The other Kurd, the one who'd tried to stop him, was jabbering away in Dari, the Kurdish dialect of Farsi, while bowing and trying to kiss Saxon's mud-spattered boots. Rempt translated, something about how Allah might bless him for saving them all with his quick thinking.

Saxon's response was to kick the sniveling Kurd in the face, shattering his nose, and walking away as the injured hillman howled in pain.

All Saxon knew was this: These shits had fucked up.

They could not be trusted. They were a liability and Marine Force One did not need liabilities—there were far too many on this mission already.

Sometime later, the Antonov set down on a desert runway marked by luminous green chemlights. The Spetsnaz commander ordered his crew to start offloading the cargo onboard the *vafl'a*—which meant "Flying Dick," a Russian nickname for any cargo aircraft—to the small convoy of waiting GAZ deuce-and-a-halfs that rested near the airstrip.

While this was taking place, there was one other detail to which he had been instructed to attend.

"You are Karlovich?" asked Major Ogarkov, as he compared the color photograph he had produced from his field jacket pocket with the face of the man standing before him in the night.

"Yes, *tovarisch*," answered the physicist. "You are my driver, then?"

"That is correct, *tovarisch*," replied the Spetsnaz, finishing another Sobranie and flicking it into the night. "Your bag, please."

The commander accepted the scientist's grip and stowed it in the rear of the staff car, then pulled open the door.

"Please have a seat."

"The ride will not be long?" asked Karlovich.

"No," replied Ogarkov, "it is very short. You will be able to rest and wash up in no time."

"I meant . . ."

"Ah yes, I see," Ogarkov cut in. "That is not a problem. The entire desert is yours."

Karlovich muttered something and walked off into the

night. The Spetsnaz lit another smoke and leaned against the side of the staff car as he watched the scientist disappear around a large rock formation. He took a long, deep drag and then shrugged, thinking that now was as good a time as any.

Pushing himself erect off the side of the vehicle, Ogarkov followed Karlovich's footprints in the loose sand covering the desert crust. As he reached the outcropping, the major drew his nine-millimeter Makarov PM (Pistolet Makarov) semiautomatic service pistol and casually threaded an eccentric-chamber LARAND-type silencer tuned to the specific sound dynamics of the weapon onto its muzzle.

None of his men heard the volley of rapid clicks that signaled the entry of bullets into the back of the traitor's skull. Major Ogarkov's roughened hand unthreaded the now hot silencer, dropped it into the pocket of his field jacket and reholstered the semiautomatic pistol.

Some blood spatter had gotten on his palm—he had held it upraised as a splash guard—and he wiped it clean on the sand. It was a lucky break that the traitor had a weak bladder; saved the major a trip into the night to do the job. But burying him—*ni khuya*—that was work for one of his men. The major would have no part of that.

"Ryabov! Kushkin!" he shouted toward the trucks as he two-fingered another smoke from the crushed pack in his pocket. "Get the fuck over here on the double. I have a job for you two lazy *svoloki*. . . ."

chapter *eight*

Saxon walked through the *mostazafin* encampment, feeling the hostile eyes of the Peshmerga upon him. He was on his way to Rempt's yurt to be briefed on new developments concerning MF-1's mission in the Elburz. Just ahead of Saxon, a group of pancake-hatted and turbaned men carrying Kalashnikovs had congregated, and it was clear by their glances and gestures that Saxon was the topic of conversation.

It was also clear they weren't paying him any compliments. No matter that the trigger-happy raghead would probably have signed all their death warrants by shooting at the Hinds. All that the clannish hill tribesmen knew was that Haneen had left behind a bereaved widow and five hungry children.

Far worse was the fact that Haneen had been killed by an unclean foreigner, one who fucked dogs, as it was said of Americans. The hands of an American infidel had snapped Haneen's neck, and such a death was an ignoble one.

The near-debacle at the surveillance post in the mountains had marked a clear turning point in MF-1's mission. From that point on the shit had begun hitting the fan with a vengeance. Tensions in the Kurdish encampment had been inflamed by the loss of one of their own people. Rempt had intervened with the *khadkhuda*, the Peshmerga tribal council, to restore order with some success, but it was obvious that the blood of the Kurds was up and a thirst for vengeance went unslaked.

Rempt had come down hard on Saxon, blaming him for having stirred up a hornet's nest.

"There was no other way," Saxon had protested. "What was I to do, let him fire? The fucker was disobeying orders. There was no other choice. I had to take him out."

"They told me you were a hardcase," Rempt said. "They warned me you were a crazy motherfucker. That you were out of control."

"You didn't answer my question," Saxon replied.

Rempt repeated his meaningless catechism about Saxon being crazy, out of control, and several other things besides.

Now Saxon would notify Rempt that he was pulling his people out. For Marine Force One the mission was over, and fuck the CIA.

As Saxon continued on the winding path up the hillside to Rempt's yurt, the group of hostile hillmen moved toward him. They now blocked Saxon's path. One of them stuck out his hand, giving Saxon the finger.

"*Charra alaik!* American fuck! *Charra alaik!*"

He spat on the ground, keeping his black button eyes glued on Saxon's face. He was saying "Shit on you" in

Dari. The other men began circling, moving out of Saxon's direct field of view.

Saxon gave the leader the finger right back. He knew a few choice words in Dari himself. *"Coos!"* he shouted. *"Tal hazi zib umak!"* This meant, "Fuck you. Call your mother over to suck my dick."

"Telhazi teezi—Go suck my ass," shouted back the Kurd. *"Coos*, American. *Coos! Coos!"*

"Coos yourself, shitbag."

Saxon looked around for a rock to throw at the evil-smelling, foulmouthed, rag-clad hillmen whom he had come to regard by now as little more than a noisy species of two-legged, humanoid cockroach, when he caught a flash of movement in his peripheral vision.

Before the raghead to Saxon's left could bring the butt of his Kalashnikov down against the side of his skull, Saxon pivoted, sidestepped the blow and launched a spinning *giri* at the attacker's heart region. The karate foot blow shattered the Kurd's collarbone and sent him sprawling to the ground.

Saxon was already centered on the follow-through, turning to face the vengeful cousin who had raised his Kalashnikov to fire a burst into Saxon's chest. As the cousin pulled the trigger, Saxon grabbed a knife-wielding raghead by the beard and one arm and heaved him around right into the line of fire.

The cousin's automatic burst punched a ragged hole in the hillman's stomach. Saxon launched another foot blow and knocked the rifle to the ground. A couple of well-placed punches to the cousin's face reduced his nose and cheeks to red, pulpy custard. The would-be killer howled in pain as he tried to hold his busted nose together amid the blood pouring out of his smashed septum, then ran off into the encampment.

The staccato sounds of automatic fire made all the parties to the brawl turn and look up at the source of the sudden report. Rempt stood outside his yurt on a rock ledge about thirty feet above them. He clutched a Kalashnikov in his right hand, barrel upraised.

The beard-and-turban contingent picked up their wounded and limped off, muttering curses in their local dialect and directing angry looks at Saxon.

Saxon walked on, reaching Rempt on the precipice above, still clutching his AKS just outside his yurt.

"What the hell was that about?"

"Take a wild guess. A couple of ragheads ambushed me on the way over. One of them said he was the cousin of the clown I had to take out. He said they were going to do some nasty things to my pecker with their knives."

"Shit, fuckin' shit," Rempt cursed. "Just what we need here. A vendetta. I want you to know I hold you responsible, Saxon. If you hadn't—"

"Hadn't what, Rempt?" Saxon had taken two steps toward the spook and grabbed him by the collar. "I've taken enough crap from you and from them. What I came here to tell you, my friend, is that I'm pulling my force out of this quagmire as of oh-three-hundred hours."

"You can't do that." Rempt had squirmed free of Saxon's grip by this time. "I'm in command of this operation."

"You're in command of diddly-squat, Rempt," Saxon shouted back. "I don't take my orders from you. I, and my forces, only liaise with you. My orders come down through the military chain of command, and you're not one of the links." Saxon reached into his shirt pocket. "This is a printout from Washington."

Rempt read the telex, which had been delivered over

satellite downlink less than an hour before. The orders stated that Major Saxon would keep his force in-theater at his own discretion.

"Unless you have a very good reason to the contrary I'm yanking my people out of this hellhole in three hours."

Rempt stood dumbfounded for a few minutes, his eyes darting to and fro. Here was a guy whose mental gears you could almost see turning inside his skull, thought Saxon.

"OK, look," he said. "I can contest these orders. The DCI will have one of his deputies camping out in front of the Oval Office before the page comes out of the printer at Meade. But I agree that your mission's been compromised by the events of last night and MF-1 should pull out. Except not tonight."

"Why not?"

"Tonight is important," Rempt said. "Tonight is the culmination of a lot of behind-the-scenes work. Trust me, Saxon. We have to do this."

"I'd sooner trust a rattlesnake. Convince me."

Rempt tried. Saxon listened to the intelligence field asset talk about the planned mission. Another mission up in the hills of the Elburz watching big Russian planes dance on the thermals. But it was more than watching this time. Much more.

The plan was pure spook. Insane. Yet it was precisely the kind of operation that would in fact have the DCI's hatchetmen camping out on the White House lawn if necessary. Saxon knew this for sure. Were he to balk and insist on extraction, Rempt would make his calls and the 1-Patchers' orders would change.

"Let's assume I were to agree to keep the force in this shithole another twenty-four hours, Rempt," Saxon began.

"What would keep the whole camp from going ballistic? You saw what happened on my way over. The Kurds have their tits in an uproar. They won't let it alone."

"You leave that to me," Rempt advised. "I'll handle it."

Saxon told Rempt that he doubted he could, but he would keep MF-1 in-theater an additional twenty-four hours in order to conduct the night's final mission into the Elburz.

"There's something else besides," Saxon added. "In my opinion the entire support operation here's been compromised. Those Hinds last night—I don't think they just happened to be there by coincidence. I think the Russians knew, or suspected, that something was shaking."

"That'll be my problem too, Saxon," Rempt answered. "After tonight's mission you and your force will be history."

Something about the look in Rempt's cold blue eyes as he said that gave Saxon the creeps. It could just be common, garden variety spookery—every one of them had a streak of James Jesus Angleton in his soul—but then, again, maybe it was more than that. Saxon would keep his guard up, and pass the word to his men.

T he night mission proceeded on schedule. Their fearless leader Rempt had been true to his word, after a fashion. He had succeeded in quelling the fires of discontent in the encampment, but the uneasy truce between tribesmen and Marines had been bought rather than negotiated.

Rempt had dug into his Company imprest fund and paid off the tribal *khadkhuda* in fifty-dollar gold pieces. He had also promised a new consignment of better weapons at the next air drop. But first came the mission.

As with the last mission into the heights of the Elburz range, the mixed force was deployed along the rocky ledges and jagged outcroppings of the bottleneck, awaiting the next clandestine resupply run out of Kharkov. Only this time there were a few wrinkles that had not been in evidence during the previous mission.

One of these wrinkles was not even present in the operational area at all. On the contrary, it was parked in low earth orbit some hundred miles above the action. It was a satellite that bore the code name Cerberus, and it differed from most other satellites in that it was mostly a huge rectangle, about the size of a trailer, filled with wet-cell electrical storage batteries.

Another wrinkle in the night's operation was a tubular weapon that was mounted on a tripod. The tube did not fire a projectile of any kind, however. Instead, a series of cables ran from the rear of the tube to a regulated power source and an electronic device housed in a milspec-hardened carrying case. Rempt had set up the rig himself, calibrating the weapon by means of a head-mounted display that was plugged into the central processing unit.

The rest was standard operating procedure. The team got into position well in advance of the expected arrival of the airborne shuttle run and settled down to wait in the darkness and biting cold of the arid, windswept heights.

Time ticked by, and then the first satellite warnings of the approach of the Antonov came over the downlink, and the ghost images of overhead thermal surveillance appeared on the tactical computer screens of the ambush force.

Saxon crouched in the darkness of the windswept heights, overlooking the rift valley below him, waiting for the plane to come gliding in. As was the case previously, Marine Force One was strung out around the north face of the cliffs above the yawning ravine, ready to intervene with rocket and small arms fire if the situation demanded aggressive response.

Rempt stared transfixed at the screen of the battlefield computer station, his fingers poised above the keyboard.

Soon the distant drone of the Antonov heavy-lifter's huge, shoulder-mounted jet engines was heard in the distance. The sound grew louder as the plane approached. The sound became a deafening roar as the winged metallic leviathan appeared, incredibly low over the top of the bluffs, and glided across the chasm that opened beyond, beginning its overflight of the rift valley.

Rempt paid the plane no attention. His eyes followed the computer's tracking window that showed the satellite view of the oncoming aircraft. Above the window, digital readouts showed the Antonov's altitude, course heading, velocity and other statistics. The most important of these numbers to Rempt, however, was the readout whose flashing numerics had begun steadily rolling down toward the zero mark.

Rempt might just as well have kept his eyes on the plane, because the entire procedure was automated and out of his control. When the flashing numerals counted down to zero, an attack sequence was automatically initiated.

High overhead in low earth orbit, the hundreds of power cells that had been charging with current now released the charge into a step-up transformer that increased the voltage by a factor of twenty.

The thousand kilovolts of electromagnetic energy generated by Cerberus began streaming from the projector dish pointing earthward. The EMP projector was in tickle mode, however. The electromagnetic pulse could be unleashed on ground or airborne targets in a variety of

modes, some more severe than others. In tickle mode, the
main beam was broken up into a series of smaller, less
powerful pulses. The intended effect was to compromise,
but not permanently damage, the electronic and electrical
systems of the target.

The pulses of electromagnetic energy played across the
airframe of the Antonov as it entered the airspace above
the arid gorge. The precise point along the trajectory of
the aircraft at which the pulses would begin to strike had
been calculated by earth- and space-based computers so
that the Antonov's autopilot, manual control systems, radio and backup systems would fail, yet leave the pilot
with enough room to land the plane on the floor of the
ravine.

Now, as the scenario played itself out, these calculations made thousands of miles away by shirtsleeved intelligence staff wired on coffee jags and hunched over
computer terminals studying animated simulations of the
operation, these calculations in the service of ends that
only a handful of individuals with high security clearances
knew in full, these calculations were about to become reality.

The Antonov's onboard systems began to fail as the
invisible shock waves penetrated its hull, entered the wir-
ing and overloaded integrated circuitry. Inside the cockpit,
the navigational screens and gauges began erratically
flashing. Emergency backup systems fared no better. The
pilot had no choice—or rather, he was only left with one.

"We are experiencing massive systems failure," he reported over the secure radio, breaking silence in the emergency. "Backup systems are going too. We must land
immediately."

In the cockpit of the lead Mi-24 Hind gunship that had
followed the transport plane a half mile behind, the pilot

only caught a fraction of the garbled message. But it, and the view through his forward-looking infra-red head-up display, that showed the huge plane dropping altitude as it struggled to keep its nose up, was enough. The Antonov would need to make an emergency landing. That or crash.

"Damn the luck," Captain Josip Panshin, the pilot, said to his copilot, seated back of him in the elevated weapons system officer's cockpit. "Of all the God-forsaken places to have to land a plane, it's here."

"What do we do about this?" Vanya Petrovsky in helotwo put in over the radio net. "This isn't supposed to be happening."

"We land and call Kharkov for further instructions, that's what we do, Vanya. Don't ask stupid questions. We don't even know if they'll make it down safely at this point. Nothing we can do now except wait and see."

The two Hinds hovered and danced in the black air as their crews watched the spectacle unfolding below them. The Hinds were unaffected by Cerberus, because the space-based EMP projector was capable of focusing on extremely narrow beamwidths and precisely tracking its targets. The OPPLAN crafted by nameless operatives in windowless rooms in secret offices on the Washington Beltway did not call for the helos to be disabled.

Another part of the OPPLAN had been crafted specifically for the Hinds, however. That part would be activated soon. In the meantime, the OPPLAN called for the big cargo plane to land safely. Every precaution had been taken to insure that the Russian flight deck crew had enough clearance to accomplish this feat.

Without knowing it, the Antonov's crew carried out its part of the plan almost flawlessly, the pilot putting down the flaps on the still-functional hydraulic controls to yank up the plane's nose and bring it to an emergency landing mere feet from the sheer wall of the cliff face at the opposite end of the gorge.

Once the Antonov was down, the second phase commenced. Small metallic circles positioned along the straps of Rempt's HUD fit close to the temples and crown of the skull, and a projecting flap fit close against the center of his forehead.

There were twin grips at the rear of the tubular weapon that Rempt now positioned in the general direction of the Antonov, and as the two Hinds set down nearby, Rempt activated the weapon by moving a virtual mouse cursor keyed to his eye movement across the visual field of the HUD and clicking the cursor with a double blink on the appropriate button.

Rempt instantaneously felt the weapon vibrate as the amplification circuitry was activated, and a beam of invisible force streamed from the psychotronic projector. The weapon was the end product of a half century of clandestine research and development. In the early stages of development, only the USSR had taken the concept seriously, but during the Cold War the U.S. had realized the military potential of psychotronics and pushed to close the gap in the way an earlier generation had closed a nuclear missile gap.

Although the hows and whys of the technology were still poorly understood, enough was known to produce a variety of useful weapon systems, mainly for clandestine warfare. One major difference between psychotronic beams and more conventional beams, such as laser or microwave radiation, is that psychotronic beams cannot be stopped or deflected by any known force or substance.

The projector Rempt fired sent its energies straight through the Antonov's hull, and its effects were immediate. In the same way that the electromagnetic pulse from

Cerberus had neutralized the Antonov's electronic systems, so psychotronic attack had unplugged the crew members' brains and central nervous systems. After a few seconds' exposure, the crew sat motionless in their seats, cut off from all experience of the world around them.

Rempt then turned the projector on the two descended Hinds. The weapon produced the identical result on the four crewmen in the double cockpits of the Soviet gunships. Brainwave analysis by the weapon's remote scanning sensors showed that the targets had been completely overcome by the weaponized force. Rempt then deactivated the weapon and removed the HUD.

"They're out of it," he told Saxon with unconcealed relish. "And, partner, we are going in."

chapter *nine*

Slowly, cautiously, as though approaching a trio of tranquilized prehistoric monsters, the concealed commandos and rebel forces emerged from hiding places amid the crags and crevices of the tableland and moved toward the silent, immobilized aircraft.

The tableau was surreal, yet there it was. Saxon's troops approached with weapons drawn and unsafed.

"Man, they're sure as shit out of it," Hirsh commented. "They're like zombies."

"Rempt, how deep are they under?" asked Saxon.

Saxon's squad had surrounded the two choppers and Saxon had opened the cockpit compartment door to peer inside at the pilot.

"Deep as you can get," Rempt answered as he put on a pair of padded leather gloves. "Watch this."

Hauling back and bunching his fist, the spook suddenly launched a savage right directly into the center of the pilot's face. Hot dark blood jetted from the shattered nose.

Saxon grabbed Rempt's hand and spun him around.

"You do that again and I'll break your jaw, so help me, you sick son of a bitch."

Rempt struggled loose, and his toothy smile returned to his long, lean, Texan's face.

"Don't worry, partner," he told Saxon. "One shot's all I allow myself. But these guys are history anyway, so what's the difference?" Rempt began removing the flight helmets of the first Hind's aircrew.

"It's hard to resist. It's like being on a drug high and thinking you're God, that you can do anything to any-body, but here it's true. I could cut them to pieces and they wouldn't know or feel a thing. Their nervous systems are just—unplugged's the best word, I guess."

"Rempt," Saxon said, "if this is what war's becoming in the twenty-first century, then I'd just as soon buy the farm right now. What I'm seeing disgusts me."

"Relax, you self-righteous bastard," Rempt said back. "These weapons have been around for decades. They've never been produced for the battlefield and probably never will be. There are already secret treaty protocols banning their use. But in the case of covert operations, well, that's another story entirely. In this here sandbox, any game that works, you play."

By now Rempt had removed the first flight helmet, in-serted a thin charge of plastic explosive and a micro-miniature remote detonator, and placed the helmet back onto the pilot's head.

"This poor bastard's all done," he announced, after wip-ing away the blood. He'd probably come out of it without even a sore nose. "Now let's take good care of the second pilot."

Rempt turned and walked off into the darkness, toward the other downed gunship.

* * *

Meanwhile other members of the force were conducting their part of the operation at the downed Antonov. Here too, the flight crew was completely immobilized, although there was no attempt made to tamper with any of the personnel as Rempt had done to the crew of the Hind.

On the contrary, the attention of the force was given over to the palleted and lashed-down cargo that had been carried onboard the huge heavy-lift transport aircraft. Squads of specially equipped 1-Patcher personnel swarmed over the crash-landed Soviet aircraft, some devoting their attention to the exterior hull, others entering the plane's cavernous interior.

The detail that went into the plane immediately set up generator-powered high-intensity lamps that lit the Antonov's cargo bay in a bright, hard glare. While they unshipped videocams and set about recording the specifics of the war materials that were stowed onboard the transport out of Kharkov, those stationed outside in the cold and darkness were treated to the eerie spectacle of ghost lights gleaming from within the crashlanded jet.

While the videocam crews swept through the Antonov cargo area, technicians went to work on the lashed, pelleted and crated payload onboard the heavy lifter. These crews were equipped with NBC agent detectors and precision tools of various types. Crates were opened and the cargo carefully videorecorded, some components removed where necessary.

In the case of the heavy-caliber artillery tubes that were lashed down the length of the Antonov's cavernous cargo area, these were uncrated and then subjected to a metallurgical sampling procedure. A specially modified drill was used to extract a few millimeters of metal from the tube casings, then the tubes were re-crated and lashed into their original positions.

By the time the operation at the Antonov's landing site was completed, the squad operating on and in the vicinity of the two immobilized Hind helicopter gunships had already finished up its work. The area around the Hinds had been carefully and thoroughly sanitized of all human presence, and the special forces personnel prepared to withdraw back into concealment at the base and summit of the bluffs prior to commencement of the second phase of operations.

Rempt was back behind the projector, this time inducing the reverse of the neural paralysis that had disabled the Soviet aircrew at the bottom of the gorge. Other elements of the covert mission unit monitored the ostensibly secure radio frequencies used for communications between the helos and the transport plane, using a duplicate made from Soviet radio equipment captured or copied during other missions.

Still others, including Saxon, watched intently through night observation devices as the Soviets returned to normal consciousness, albeit with no recollection of what had taken place in the approximately two hours during which the operation had been conducted.

All clocks onboard the Hinds had been reset to only a few seconds after the time that the helos had set down on the sandy floor of the ravine. The Mi-24s' systems, unlike those of the Antonov, had not been subjected to electromagnetic pulse attack, and so had remained undamaged. The covert ops technical squad onboard the Antonov had confirmed that its onboard clock had been permanently disabled, while its radio gear, which was specially hardened against EMP effect, remained functional.

Among the aftereffects of the induced neural incapacitation was no memory of missing time for those affected. The Hind aircrew, and the Antonov flight crew, both believed that they had set their aircraft down only moments before.

"Juliet Bravo, this is X-Ray Lima One. Report your status please."

The pilot of the lead chopper had radioed the crashed Antonov, requesting its crew to state its condition.

X-Ray Lima One, we have experienced massive systems failure of unknown origin which has crippled our navigational and propulsion systems. We retain marginal systems function, including radio and satcom. Fortunately, the crew seems unhurt."

"I copy, Juliet Bravo," said the Hind flight leader. "Do you believe that the aircraft can be made operational again so that a takeoff can be attempted?"

"Negative," replied the Antonov's pilot. "The plane not only sustained systems damage, but damage to the airframe on landing, including nosegear. This bird isn't going anywhere."

"I copy," said the gunship pilot. "In that case we must fall back on our emergency instructions," he went on. "Am I correct that you have no injured requiring medical evacuation assistance?"

"Yes. We can all make it under our own power. Have you enough room onboard?"

"We'll manage," replied the helo pilot, glad at least that the capacious Hinds were as much troop transport as gunship. "How soon can you evacuate? The damned *dushman*—hill bandits—might have seen something and start nosing around. The sooner we leave the better."

"I have already begun to evacuate. As soon as we destroy code books I and my copilot will follow. Out."

The Soviets aboard the two Hind gunships could already see crew members exiting from the Antonov. Fortunately there were not many personnel aboard this flight, for security and other reasons. Also fortunately, the big gunships had a great deal of extra carrying capacity.

The lead pilot checked his flight manifest, quickly punching calculations into the onboard computer for the increased rate of fuel consumption due to the extra weight the two helos would have to carry all the way to Kharkov. He nodded as he saw that there would be a slim but acceptable margin for safety, even enough to compensate for some additional delay in flight time.

As the pilot continued to watch the rest of the Antonov aircrew emerge from the stricken plane, he made further calculations, which showed that the helos would be well inside Soviet airspace before their fuel reserves had run two-thirds dry.

Here too the results looked encouraging. The new Hinds were equipped for air-to-air refueling. Immediately upon reentering Soviet airspace, he would radio for a fuelbird to meet the inbound flight and refill their tanks. The plan seemed workable.

He informed his frontseater—like many combat helos, including the U.S. Cobra, the pilot sat behind and above the weapons systems officer—of the good news over helo interphone and then again broke radio silence to inform his wingman.

Knowing that further radio communications would be necessary to coordinate the liftoff anyway, he also informed the wingman of what needed to be done per the emergency evacuation plan.

The helos would take on their passenger load and then

lift off. At their translation altitude of approximately sixty feet, the helos would move into attack formation and fire rocket salvos down into the Antonov, reducing it and its cargo to burning wreckage.

They would then get the hell out of there as fast as possible, knowing that the *dushman* would certainly come to investigate after that, if they were not on their way already.

In darkness and silence, the hidden forces waited and watched. Saxon had been assured by Rempt that the indigenous fighters, the Peshmerga, the Mujahideen, and the other categories of rebels, guerillas and true-believers, had been put in their place and would not panic.

To make sure of this, the Marines had divested their *mostazafin* allies of all rocket launchers prior to moving out to the Elburz. Saxon still had strong misgivings about permitting them to be in on the mission at all, no matter what Rempt's assurances.

They were loose cannons, all of them, stoned on religion or hashish or Marxism or the revolutionary flavor of the week. Still, they hadn't yet made a false move, and it would all be over soon.

Saxon turned his full attention to the activities taking place at the flat, sandy floor of the steep-walled gorge. The main rotors of the Hind gunships were dishing now, as the last of the evacuated Antonov aircrew got onboard the two attack helos. They remained stationary as final preparations, including a last-minute flight check, were conducted.

And then, almost in tandem, the two heavily laden helicopters rose sluggishly up off the valley floor and straight up into the air.

Saxon glanced sideward at Rempt as the Hinds reached their translation altitudes and then changed the rotor pitch to move slightly apart, pivoting their noses in the direction of the downed airframe.

As Saxon had expected, Rempt's face was again transfigured by a form of twisted rapture, the mouth contorted into a strange, rictuslike smile, the eyes focused on the screen of the battlefield computer station as Rempt's hands hovered over the tactical computer's keyboard.

The Soviet helos continued to hover slant-range of the Antonov, and Saxon knew that the battle management systems onboard were reading sensor input and calculating firing solutions for the AT-2 Swatter missiles carried on rails at the tips of their stub wings. Moments continued to pass, and then the first of the missiles cooked off the rails, coming off the helos belching contrails of dense white exhaust smoke as they vectored in on their target.

The first salvo hit with a wallop. Striking the airframe fore and aft, and exploding immediately, the warheads caused a massive double explosion that vaporized much of the plane in a balloon of flame and smoke that rose up in a mushroom cloud over the top of the bluffs.

The helos fired another two-rocket salvo into the burning wreckage, completing the job of destruction. After the fires died out, there would be little left of the Antonov and its secret cargo except a debris field of shattered fragments strewn across the rift valley floor.

The AN-72 transport now destroyed on the ground, the two Hinds rose still higher, soaring toward the top of the bluffs from which they would fly nap of the earth on a north-northeast bearing back toward Soviet airspace.

Would have flown, more precisely, because the Hinds never got farther than the crest of the bluffs.

Just before they would have changed main rotor pitch

and translated to forward flight, Rempt used the computer's integrated pointer to click on the detonator button. Instantaneously, a powerful microwave beam activated the miniature radio-actuated detonator-ignitors inserted into the sheets of plastic explosive with which he had earlier lined the flight helmets of the Hind pilots.

The small explosive charges imploded the skulls of the pilots of both gunships, spattering the cockpits with blood, bone matter and optical gore from eyeballs which had been blown clear out of their sockets due to intracranial overpressure. Death spasms induced by traumatic shocks to the central nervous systems wrenched the cyclical and collective controls, making the helos career wildly through the sky.

In any event they would have crashed against either the steep walls of the bluffs or the rift valley floor—computer projections run on the NSA's powerful Cray mainframes had demonstrated this result with nearly a hundred percent certainty. But the best outcome was what the analysts had dubbed the "Rice Bowl scenario," referring to the debacle elsewhere in the Iranian desert at another secret LZ known as Rice Bowl.

Here, a quarter century before, two Marine Sea Stallion helicopters crashed together on dust-off after the abortive attempt to free the American hostages from the U.S. embassy in Tehran was abruptly canceled.

The NSA had then utilized the "Rice Bowl Scenario" to good effect in order to protect secret assets that an extraction of U.S. personnel would have compromised. The embassy hostages were never intended to be freed— the NSA had projected that the mission would end in embarrassing failure, seriously undermining the incoming Reagan administration's foreign policy effectiveness.

It therefore had to be stopped. Cold.

On this night, decades later, the scenario would be used again in the service of other clandestine operational ends.

As the scenario played itself out, the two Soviet helicraft pitched wildly toward one another, moving so quickly that the action was almost missed in the midair explosion and blossoming fireball that immediately followed the collision.

The bluffs flashed with intense, hellish light, as sparking from the collision ignited fuel lines, and even the protective circuits in the advanced GEN-IV night vision devices used by the strike force did not totally protect the hidden watchers from the blinding glare of NVG bloomout effect.

A split-second behind the detonation flashes, the blast wave followed, booming and echoing back and forth across the walls of the steep chasm like peals of unearthly thunder.

As the fireball continued to burn in midair, spinning, whirling chunks of pulverized, vaporized wreckage cascaded downward to the flat of the valley floor, there to join the debris field of the destroyed Antonov in a memorial to covert death.

Soon the last of the echoes of man-made thunder died away, leaving only the crackling and popping of the flames burning in the ash-filled cauldron of the arid valley. The hidden watchers were silent for a moment, and then, emerging from concealed crevices amid the south wall of the bluffs, there arose a chorus of hoarse cheers from the throats of the hill tribesmen.

As the *mostazafin* shouted, they aimed their Kalashnikovs at the stars and fired off bursts of automatic fire into the air.

Saxon felt a crawling repugnance. The tribesmen had nothing to celebrate. They had played no part in the drama. They had risked nothing, done nothing, been noth-ing to the mission. His only desire now was to get the hell out of this place, and as soon as possible.

Saxon gave the order for the teams to pack up their gear and move back to their staging area, where a Marine security detail was keeping an eye on the perimeter. Rempt was already overseeing a team of Peshmerga who were packing his specialized spook gear into the same milspec-hardened carrying cases in which it had been car-ried into the mountains.

The teams now began to file from their hiding places and march toward the staging area. Here, the vehicles that had formed the team's transport convoy were taken from the two large desert wadis in the hills high above the desert in which they had been parked and kept well con-cealed under roving guard patrols throughout the duration of the operation.

Because of the strong probability of Iranian interven-tion, the convoy would split up and take preplanned routes toward the cross-border regions, across which they would dart to the mission's hideouts inside Turkey.

Before moving out, however, Saxon ordered a mobile scout platoon to strike out a mile ahead of the main mo-torized force and act as an advance warning detail. If Saxon's pickets saw evidence of enemy movement across the line of advance, they were to report back to Saxon immediately and new plans would be made.

Saxon issued final orders, gave the scout platoon a head start, and then signaled the convoy to get rolling. Lights out, the vehicles pushed out across the desert, into the moonless blackness of the night.

chapter *ten*

In fact, the covert action in the Elburz mountains had not gone unnoticed by the Iranians. Under the circumstances, it would have been surprising if it hadn't been detected by Pasdaran, or Iranian military, forces, or even by civilian outposts in the desolate borderlands.

To the covert planners, the noise and flash of the explosions had posed a calculated risk. The risk had been reduced by the apparently accidental detonation of an oil well at the nearby petroleum fields of Siphan Dagi, in southeastern Turkey, at approximately the same time as the destruction of Soviet airframes was taking place in the Elburz tablelands. But the risk couldn't be removed entirely.

Still, the deception had worked, and it had worked effectively. The mysterious detonations that preceded the ignition of the well (its source would never be conclusively determined), sending immense contrails of flame and smoke geysering high into the atmosphere, were heard hundreds of miles away, across the Iranian border in the key military outposts at the provincial capital, Tabriz. The oil explosions had masked the triple aircraft kills so well that nothing about the true action in the Elburz was suspected by Iranian forces.

Consequently, no tripwire forces had been mobilized to investigate the strange thunder and lightning in the mountains. Mobile troops were occupied elsewhere, conducting normal night operations. Instead, the mission was compromised by pure chance.

A lone Iranian motorized patrol making its way across the desert simply happened to see a remote series of flashes from a direction other than that of the blasts at Siphan Dagi.

Had the patrol not been in its precise position on the desert at that precise moment in time, it might have missed the flashes, but it was and so it hadn't.

"We've just observed evidence of an attack," the patrol leader had radioed to base.

"No, you are mistaken," he'd been informed. "A major oil well fire is burning across the border in Turkey. This is certainly what you have seen."

"Impossible," the patrol leader replied. "What I saw came from an entirely different direction—in the Elburz."

"You mean what you *think* you saw." The voice of the base commander fell silent a moment while he thought things over. "Is there continued activity?"

"No. Nothing more."

"Then resume patrol."

"Sir, I—"

"You have your orders, Captain. Obey them."

And the Iranian captain did as ordered. Except not quite in the way he had been instructed by his superior officer. He knew old Manoucheher as a drunken slob who buggered sheep in his drunken off-hours, at least so went the rumor. He also knew that he had seen what he had seen and heard what he had heard, and fuck Manoucheher on a camel's ass.

The captain knew the desert landscape quite well, having conducted many an exercise and patrol by day and by night across an area encompassing hundreds of square miles.

He was aware that the most passable routes away from the Elburz ran roughly east-west and were not far from his current position. Further, in this part of the Iranian desert, motorized travel for any distance needed to keep to the road, further limiting the search area.

He would deviate his patrol just far enough to avoid charges of dereliction of duty, yet neatly circumvent the major's orders. With any luck, he would come upon something of interest. Something that might lead to the action he had so long craved.

"**B**oss, company's comin'."
      Cherokee, which was Lieutenant Frisky's scout patrol, had just reported in. Cherokee had been conducting its flank security operations about twenty miles ahead and to the southwest of the main force element, staying off the road and stopping periodically to reconnoiter.

"Am ID'ing an Iranian Pasdaran scout patrol, probably out on night ops. We're laying low and watching them roll by on the road. Wait one."

There was dead air as Lieutenant Frisky paused to check the image on his thermal scope against what he could see with unaided night vision.

"Enemy force strength is about forty troops. These guys are in two BTR-70s with a GAZ scout car up front. Be advised they're heading directly towards you."

Saxon didn't like what he'd heard. He figured that the explosions in the mountains had been noticed despite diversionary precautions. Still, this had been a possibility all along.

"Can you take them out?"

"Negative," Lieutenant Frisky answered right off. "We could try but I'd prefer not to go up against those BTRs with the two rocket launchers we have available."

Saxon acknowledged and issued orders. An ambush would be set up. It would be a kill basket with Lt. Frisky's patrol closing any rear exit. The main force element would take up positions at either side of the road—Saxon had kept his eyes open for good ambush sites along the route out of long habit, and had noticed a likely spot only a few hundred yards back.

Within a matter of minutes, the force had moved skillfully and silently to position its vehicles off and away from the desert road, while men armed with small arms and rocket launchers, including the heavy Dragon and smaller-caliber SMAW, took up positions on either side.

The ground here sloped down from the road, which had been laid right across part of a large wadi. In bulldozing the road, the builders had simply built up an embankment for the asphalt surfacing. The earthworks sloped away into the hollow of the wadi on both sides.

Men armed with rocket launchers and automatic weapons could effectively position themselves to bring intersecting fields of enfilading fire and high explosive strikes down on a target in between without much threat to their own safety, since the fire lanes would be directed upward on the diagonal.

Once the ambush teams were in position, Saxon waited and watched, ready to issue the order to commence firing on the enemy troops. MF-1 had to strike fast and score clean kills. It was imperative that they prevent the Iranians from reporting the contact via radio.

An unfriendly patrol was one thing, but Saxon's force would not survive direct engagement with a brigade-strength detachment, and such is what the Iranians would send out to comb the desert if an alert came in. It would include helos, APCs and a lot of troops.

In the visual field of the binocular night vision scope strapped to his head beneath his Fritz helmet, Saxon saw the unfriendly patrol emerge onto his event horizon.

"Safe fire until I signal," he reminded his unit commanders, whispering into his lipmike.

The enemy scout patrol continued to roll closer to the narrow end of the killbox. Saxon's right hand tightened on the trigger grip of his SMAW anti-armor missile launcher and his pulse quickened. The moment to attack was drawing near.

But then, suddenly, the tactical picture changed.

The scout patrol, rolling into the jaws of the waiting trap like a bit of iron drawn irresistibly toward a magnet, stopped without warning. Its commander then stood atop the rear seat of the scout car and raised a pair of night-seeing binoculars to his face.

Holding the light-amplifying field glasses, he moved his upper torso to and fro, sweeping the binocs around in a wide arc. Like a pendulum swinging back, he began to return the binoculars to their starting point. With relief, Saxon watched him begin to lower the field glasses. He had seen nothing. . . .

Saxon's judgment proved premature. In a second, as if to confirm something he had noticed earlier, the young Pasdaran captain again raised the light-amplification binoculars to his eyes and held them there for several long seconds. This time the binoculars were brought down abruptly. This time he had seen something that had convinced him not to move forward another inch.

Saxon watched with mounting alarm as the captain began issuing rapid-fire orders for the troops in the first BTR to emerge from the armored war wagon and fan out along the part of the road that spanned the wadi. Now MF-1's commander suspected what the Iranian officer had seen to change his plans so drastically. Like Saxon, he too had noticed that the sides of the road were ideally sited for an ambush point and had decided to deploy a squad of crunchies to reconnoiter before the patrol continued along the road.

Saxon's mind whirled like the hard drive of a computer as he mentally processed options to deal with the emerging FUBAR situation. He selected the only workable option from his mental checklist and prepared to put the plan into action.

"Gusher, Crash. Don't answer. Listen. On my three count get on your feet and fire your rockets at the patrol. Gusher takes the scout car. Crash takes the first BTR. I'll take the second BTR." Saxon paused a beat, and the mental hard drive spun some more.

"All unit commanders, listen up—when you see us fire, give us two seconds to duck back down again, then open up with everything you got."

Saxon began counting down, from three to zero. On the final count, he jumped up, seeing Gusher and Crash do the same from their positions. Sighting the crosspiece of the SMAW's pancake scope on his target, he triggered the forty-millimeter rocket projectile, feeling the launcher tube kick like a mule on his shoulder from the recoil of the backblast, and hearing the whoosh of the rocket's contrail like a steam pipe had just burst next to his right ear.

Time slowed in the familiar way it does in the heat of combat, and Saxon's visual field turned into a kind of tunnel. Down the length of that tunnel he watched the warhead streak toward its target, then impact into the armored hull of the BTR in a devastating blast of flame and concussion that blew molten fragments of steel and fused, flaming debris out from the epicenter of the blast.

As the BTR burned up on the desert, Saxon's mind also registered the second and third impacts that marked Gusher and Crash's rounds hitting their targets. His launcher spent, he ducked down again, and heard the din of battle start up all around him. Picking up his AKMS assault rifle, Saxon joined its stuttering voice to the choir of death, quickly becoming aware that the unit had a pitched battle on its hands.

Troops armed with AK-47s were attacking the ambush teams from all sides, and it fast became obvious to Saxon that the rocket strikes, while incapacitating the mobile armored patrol, had far from destroyed it or stopped its ability to counterattack.

The Iranian vehicles were halted, and many enemy had been killed and seriously wounded in the surprise strike, but others were still alive and the unfriendlies had at least one big gun still operational.

Saxon's force was now taking casualties as Iranian regulars, clad in olive-drab fatigues, began to engage them on the ground. The ambush had turned into nasty close-quarter fighting in many places, with men trading automatic fire and throwing grenades at close range.

In some cases, the fighting got even closer than that. As ammo clips were bled dry in the heat of combat, the opposing forces resorted to hand-to-hand fighting and bayonet attacks. Saxon found himself engaged in one such confrontation as a big Iranian sergeant suddenly jumped over the roadbed and launched a deft martial arts front-kick at his AKMS as he was about to reload. The bullpup rifle flew from his hands and fell with a clatter in the darkness somewhere off to his left.

The sergeant immediately went into a defensive stance as Saxon drew the long, serrated knife scabbarded at his belt. The sergeant scoffed at this and said something in Iranian, gesturing contemptuously at Saxon to advance and try his luck with the knife.

Saxon continued to circle warily. As a martial arts expert he had pegged the sergeant's movements to the native Iranian martial arts style called Zur Khane.

Zur Khane is practiced in an octagonal arena and is a style that is heavily dependent on muscular strength and stamina. The sergeant had the look of a Zur Khane practitioner, one accustomed to many confrontations in the octagon.

Again the sergeant gestured contemptuously for Saxon to lunge at him, spitting on the ground. Saxon had another idea. He flung the knife, knowing it would miss, but he used his opponent's distraction to tuck down and roll sideways for his lost rifle.

As the sergeant bore down on him, Saxon fired from a prone position on his back, emptying half his clip. At close range the burst cut the Iranian practically in half.

Saxon was up and running as his opponent fell. Amid the chaos of battle he still heard the distinct sound of the BTR's guns chattering away. Mounting to the surface of the road, he scoped out the situation. Somehow the enemy war wagon had survived multiple rocket strikes.

Bodies were piled up in front of it, however, and it was clearly mortally damaged. To make sure it would blow, Saxon ordered that jerry cans of gasoline be thrown beneath the BTR by troops covered by diversionary fire.

Once this had been done, using the last of their remaining rockets, the squads fired a final salvo.

In combination with the gasoline, the BTR began to burn, and its gun fell finally silent.

The battle was over. Dense, moonless darkness still covered the arid desert landscape.

The firefight, though intense, had been brief, and in this remote corner of the desert there was the likelihood that it had gone undetected.

However, even in the event the unfriendly patrol had never gotten off a radio distress call, with the coming of daylight its absence would be noted and a search mission would be launched.

Although Saxon's force would be long gone from the scene of battle by then, the longer discovery and identification was delayed, the better.

Saxon ordered that enemy dead be buried and the wreckage of the patrol's vehicles be pushed into the wadi and draped with camouflage netting, then covered with sand and rock to further disguise and conceal the wreckage. With any luck it would be several more days before the vanished patrol was located, and if a *shamal* blew up, the additional sand deposited by the storm might delay discovery even longer.

Once these actions were carried out, Saxon ordered the graves detail to put friendly dead in body bags and place them aboard the unit's vehicles. Because they'd parked these in hide sites well removed from the ambush site that was the major scene of the engagement with the Iranian patrol, the vehicles were completely intact.

After scout patrol squads were again sent forward as pickets, and final preparations were made, the convoy moved out again, toward its hide site across the Turkish border.

chapter *eleven*

The mission into the Elburz had been completed, but Saxon had not yet been able to extract Marine Force One as he had warned Rempt he would do on completion.

Bad weather had settled in shortly after the force's return to its borderland encampments. A period of biting cold and fierce *shamals*, blizzards that combined frozen rain, hail and sandstorms, had grounded inbound V-22 and helo flights. Until there was a hole in the weather to afford an opportunity window to extract, Saxon and his people were grounded.

This was not good. The tension in the camp, temporarily dispelled by the covert mission and the subsequent fighting withdrawal, had returned, and the adverse weather conditions had worsened flaring tempers. Saxon was still being held accountable by the Peshmerga for the killing of one of their own, and he had been warned of plans for revenge.

Not that he needed much warning: The beard-and-turban contingent was making it plain, in the way they'd done before the mission, that they were still out for blood. As far as Saxon was concerned, so be it. If the tribesman wanted another funeral or two, then that's what their sorry-assed little vendetta would cost them.

As soon as the weather cleared, he would leave the Koran-thumping assholes to the hell on earth that they and their sheep-fucking ancestors had created. Saxon understood the geopolitical realities that led America to at times cast its lot with the fucked-up nationalities of the far-flung corners of the earth, but the ground truth was another matter entirely.

That ground truth had driven American soldiers half-insane in Indochina, as members of the most advanced culture on earth were forced to live day to day with one of the most primitive. As far as Saxon went, dealing with the Peshmerga had been like taking a time trip back to the Stone Age. He'd be glad to return to civilization. Even eating fast food and breathing carbon monoxide was better than this.

Another throwback Saxon would be glad to leave behind was Rempt. Here was an especially toxic spook. In hindsight, Saxon had almost been glad to find himself engaged in actual combat during the gone-sour ambush on the road.

What had preceded it was sickness and perversity, acts unworthy of a soldier and an American. Saxon would need to wash the memory of his time in the Elburz borderlands from his mind, and he knew it had already cost him another little piece of his soul.

The weather worsened as winter storm systems marched across the face of the land. Above the thirty-fifth parallel, in the extreme north of the Mideast, the rocky, arid deserts and stony gray mountains are often swept by freezing rain, pelted by hail and scoured by blizzards of wind-driven sand.

The weather picture complicated the mission, increasing the challenges to the planning cell based at Incirlik, Turkey. They were professionals, however, and had conducted numerous clandestine paramilitary operations in the regional theater over the years.

They knew the vagaries of the region's storm systems and were certain that a window of opportunity would open up within the time frame for the operation. Plus they had some very accurate meteorological data available to them.

For the moment the biggest problem would be in keeping the operation sterile and tightly compartmentalized. The operational detachment had been taken from one of the Western European NATO countries and had been told nothing concerning the operation, other than that their objective would be the destruction of an Islamist terror group based on the eastern flank of NATO.

In operations such as these, where foreign nationals are used as surrogates, the procedure is based on the quick turnaround. The operational detachment is trained, briefed, sent out to do its job, debriefed and returned to its home nation, all within a few days' time.

Here, the delay caused by the weather posed several problems and risks. The airborne assault elements and ground forces both needed to be kept in a state of seclusion at the base near Incirlik. They could not be permitted to roam from the base.

But experience had taught the planners that even the most thoroughly indoctrinated troops can be ingenious in breaching security when claustrophobia sets in. The planners didn't like that.

It came as some relief when the chief meteorologist brought them the favorable report for which they had hoped. The operational detachment would be able to commence its assault on the target at two hundred hours. The planning cell wasted no time in bringing their end of the operation to a close.

Nightstalker was on again.

The unmarked black helicopters converged on the strike zone amid worsening weather conditions. Although the night skies had been clear when they had lifted off from Incirlik several hours before, the helo crews had encountered the tail end of a fierce *shamal* that had barreled its way across the mountains west of Tabriz like a runaway express freight.

Still, the crews had their orders. They were not to turn back unless the weather made further flight impossible. Since this was not the case, the flight leader continued on toward the target. As the gunships reached their objective, the crews turned on their recording equipment, including gun cameras, and prepared to strike.

The sandstorm that the Nightstalker gunship sortie had pushed through also began to abate as the strike mission neared its final target initial points. Within minutes the night sky was clear again, and the terrorist encampment visible on their infra-red head-up displays.

Now about a half-mile slant-range of the target, the encampment appeared almost identical to the scale models placed on sand tables that had been used to plan the mission. The primitive stone and mud-brick yurts were scattered here and there across a main compound, with several others on ledges of the adjoining mountain peaks.

Vehicles of various types, including some Land Rovers

outfitted with TOW missiles, heavy machine guns and twenty-millimeter coaxial cannons, were also in evidence, most of them concealed under camouflage netting.

Apart from this, and a lone sentry spotted smoking a cigarette on a lonely, windswept hillside, there was no evidence of activity at the terrorist encampment at 0335 hours. The terrorists would all be asleep inside the buildings, except for the sentry, and he didn't count in the overall picture.

The Nightstalker flight leader had seen enough to convince him that the mission would go down without a hitch. He flashed the thumbs-up to his copilot and signaled two clicks over the comms net to alert the other members of the sortie that they were to move into their preplanned attack vectors.

Now the helos split up and commenced the assault, the lead chopper acquiring the large central building that he was told would house an especially dangerous terrorist element. The death dot moved to the center of the crosshairs and the gunship pilot triggered a salvo of missiles that came off the sides of the chopper in two flashing bursts. White smoke contrails snaked downward, following the warheads to the points of impact.

The building went up in a ball of flame, and the pilot came off the vector, slewing the gunship out of the rising toadstool of flame and destruction that belched up into the night.

Somewhere inside that pillar of fire were the vaporized remains of the approximately twenty to twenty-five terrorists who had been asleep in that no-longer-existent barracks building. The thought sobered the pilot, but only for a second. His most important thought was that he had scored a good kill, and that's what he'd been paid to do.

The hazardous duty bonus he'd receive wouldn't hurt either.

He was also paid to die, which is what happened before his heart finished its next contraction, as a TOW missile streaked in the helo's direction. The TOW had come up off one of the parked, camouflage-netted and apparently unmanned trucks scattered throughout the encampment.

Not having taken these out first was a tactical blunder, albeit an explainable one. After all, the vehicles were thermally neutral, showing no evidence of hot spots associated with warm engines, or even human operators.

The flight leader would be able to explain the error, but only in the afterlife, if there was one, because in the blink of an eye, the TOW's shaped-charge, proximity-fuzed warhead exploded amidships, vaporizing the helo into a million flaming fragments.

The flight leader and copilot were broiled in their seats even as they reached for the ejection levers. They should have thought about what might be concealed underneath those parked vehicles: warm bodies against the cold sand, thermally insulated from above, thermally neutral to slant-range TI detection.

Now, man-portable and vehicle-mounted anti-air was coming up at the gunship sortie from every direction. Mean, lean Marine ass-kickers had been placed throughout the compound in positions of maximum surprise and tactical advantage if met by an opposing force.

There had been no "terrorists" in the buildings, only empty bunks. Saxon had deployed the Mean One and some of the hill tribesmen he could halfway trust throughout the encampment. He had smelled a stink brewing on the wind, and he had not been mistaken.

As salvos of deadly fire were traded and the ground shook under the impact of crashing flying machines and thundering missile strikes, Saxon thought back to the events of the past several hours.

A fierce *shamal* had closed in, subjecting the mountains to a mixture of wind-blasted sand and pounding hail that had gone on for hours.

During that time atmospherics had played hob with radio and satcom communications, but more than that was going on within the encampment. It started to become evident that under cover of the storm much of the insurgent force was moving off into the mountains, taking advantage of the storm's cover to hide their departure.

Saxon was about to go off in search of Rempt for an explanation when "Doc" Jeckyll, MF-1's comms officer, flagged him down. Jeckyll had gotten a momentary patch into surveillance satellite downlink. He had seen what had appeared to be a helo force approaching from the northwest. What's more, he didn't think it was only atmospherics that had ruined transmission. Jeckyll told Saxon that he thought they were being deliberately jammed.

Sensing an impending attack, Saxon issued immediate orders to the MF-1 detachment. His Marines were to drop their cocks, grab their socks and prepare to move out, overland if necessary.

Saxon explained that the extraction helos might not be coming and that they could be faced with a situation that called for SERE (search, evasion, reconnaissance and escape) procedures. But first he deployed the force in anticipation of a heliborne strike. It materialized quickly, but MF-1 was ready to confront it and prevail using ground-to-air weapons.

Returning to the present, Saxon watched another unmarked black gunship explode in the air and burst apart into a cascade of showering fragments. The team had done its work well. The sky was now clear of unfriendly air assets.

Saxon issued instructions for the team to mount up and move the hell out. Saxon would follow once he had gotten the skinny on one final matter.

As he suspected, Rempt's living quarters had been completely destroyed. The spook's yurt was a heap of smoldering wreckage. And in the midst of that wreckage, there were the charred remains of a man wearing the hill tribesman's attire that Rempt had affected.

The only thing was, Saxon was sure it wasn't Rempt. For one thing, the corpse had a broken nose. Right where Saxon had bashed it in with the steel toe of his combat boot two days before. Rempt had taken a powder. Saxon would bet his life on it.

chapter *twelve*

Marine Force One rolled, walked and bitched on into the mountains, eventually crossing from Turkey into Iran. The traversal of national borders was marked only by a cursor position on the Marines' GPS displays. There were no mile markers in these desolate borderlands, and no natural terrain features to mark the boundary lines. Just the arid hill country, the treacherous switchback road and the limpid blue stretched tight above them like a pastel plastic lid. Though Turkey was a NATO member, Saxon chose to avoid withdrawing the team through it for several reasons.

One, the covert kill-strike had come from the direction of Incirlik, and Saxon well knew that the southeastern corner of Turkey had been a spook haven since the earliest days of the Cold War.

Two, Saxon had suspected there might be trouble brewing ever since the clandestine operations in the Elburz Bottleneck.

He well knew the pattern of cold-blooded deception followed by spasmodic violence that could develop when black ops planning cells buried deep in the CIA's Directorate of Operations ran the show. The techniques had been developed and refined during the Reagan era during counter-Soviet operations in neighboring Afghanistan. Saxon knew them well, having served as a military advisor in low-intensity warfare and special weaponry to the Jamat-I-Islami mujahideen faction in mountain enclaves near Spin Gar Bor, and he also knew the way the "black minds" in those cells at Langley thought.

In the Afghan theater both the Soviets, the United States, and the Islamist third-party insurgents, were developing the tools and stratagems of twenty-first century small-unit warfare. Afghanistan was the place where West met East and both met Mideast.

While America's attention was directed to Oliver North's actions in Latin America, the new face of sub-warfare was showing itself far to the east, in the rugged mountains of this ancient battleground.

Here, both sides perfected the use of exotic weaponry such as Rempt had directed against the Soviets. Here grand deception and dispassionate manipulation of fighting cells became the first order of battle.

The pattern was familiar. Covert paramilitary teams would conduct clandestine missions. Later, other scalpel forces would be deployed to wipe out those teams so the knowledge of the events they had set in motion would be lost forever.

Compartmentalization would be airtight, but the multiplication of paramilitary cells in the war zone produced results similar to the wildfire spread of cancer cells in the human body. From that spook war in Afghanistan had emerged the Osama bin Ladens and the Hassan Ramad

Ali's of the new millennium's terrorist international, turning the United States' own secret warfare tactics against their creator.

Some of those nasty little backchannel combat campaigns begat dire consequences. The attack on the Golden Gate bridge by Ali's bloodthirsty Shadow Brigades in 2003, for example, had been one of them.

No. There would be no sanctuary in Turkey for Marine Force One.

Not yet, at least.

The *shamals* came barreling in again like a freight out of hell. The weather worsened. This time Saxon welcomed the storms as part blessing, at least, because he suspected that a second Nightstalker attack wave would be coming in behind the first covert strike teams.

The Mean One marched on through the *shamals*. The unit humped mostly by night, halting only when weather conditions became so grave as to prohibit movement entirely.

The unit kept to the high ground as much as possible. More than once, the detachment had seen flash floods completely fill large wadis in a matter of minutes. There would have been no escape from such an inundation, at least not in time to save the team's vehicles, missile launchers and critical food and ammo supplies.

Nature wasn't their only adversary. Suddenly, in the midst of clearing away debris from a rock slide that blocked their line of withdrawal, the Marines heard the sound of helicopter rotorblades somewhere slant-range of them. Saxon signaled for vehicle drivers to kill their engines and for everybody to hit the dirt. The team's Hummers were driven into any available hiding places, and the team hunkered down for cover, weapons at the ready.

They had heard and seen many helo overflights since their departure from the rebel sanctuary inside the Turkish border. The hunters were keeping up the pressure, intensively searching for the team. The first attackers had come in by helo, and while the next attack might come by land, the scalpel force would certainly use airborne patrols of some kind in an effort to track One's position.

As the team listened, waited and watched, the chugging and droning of the oncoming helos grew steadily louder. The sounds soon merged together into a single deafening roar. Somewhere, very close by and not too high overhead, the black helos were hovering, darting back and forth, listening and watching.

Like the other members of the unit strung out along the ridgeline, Saxon's fists tightened on the handgrip and underbarrel of his AKMS as he strained to catch every nuance of sound from above. The team would remain concealed if possible, but if they were fired upon, Saxon had ordered them to hit back and kill the helos with ground-to-air missile strikes.

This time the choppers began moving off, though. First one, then the other began to come off their hovers, and then the entire sequence reversed.

The steady, deafening roar of dishing rotors began to waver, to unravel into an echoing, chugging, pistoning turbulence that soon faded altogether. In minutes the helos had moved off and the threat had passed.

"You think they made us, Boss?" asked Sgt. One Eyes.

"I don't know," Saxon replied. "If these guys didn't, then the next time, or the time after that, they will. We're living on the edge, here."

"I gotcha, Boss."

Saxon had dispatched scout units to conduct security

operations on the force's flanks. He checked with them via secure radio links. Had they detected any evidence of ground forces approaching?

"Negative," replied Corporal Dibs. "We ain't seen nothing but sand, snakes and scorpions so far."

The same answer came from the two other buddy teams Saxon had out working flank patrol.

Saxon consulted his wrist chronometer. The liquid crystal digits told him that the team still had several hours of march time left before it would need to hole up with the dawn of day.

The major signaled his team to remount and move out again. Vehicle engines cranked to life and combat boots began crunching sand and gravel. Men and machines picked themselves up and once more began to march and roll and curse—straight-leg, mud-sucking infantry, doing what universal soldiers always did.

The 1-Patchers had gone to ground as the sun beat down upon the desert. They moved out again once darkness fell. They had come down out of the mountains into the flat stony desert that lies amidst the Elburz and Zagros mountain ranges between the Turkish border and Tehran.

The Iranian capital city is nestled close to the middle of the spine of the Elburz range which cuts east-west across Iran's northern tier. Tehran was still several hundred miles to the southeast. Because of the inhospitable nature of the desert here, and the fact that it has few exportable natural resources except the vast salt deposits of a fossil sea, the region is sparsely populated.

Saxon believed the odds were still in MF-1's favor for an extraction from a dot on the Iranian Kavir Desert, the

Dasht-E Kavir, in Farsi, called Manzariyah. The remote abandoned salt mine there was just within the maximum range of Marine Sea Stallions dispatched from Masirah Island off the eastern coast of Oman, known, because of its ovenlike heat and tormenting flies, as "Misery" Island.

Already Marine aviation teams were working at a makeshift airstrip on Masirah to ready the two CH-53E rescue choppers for the inbound flight. Technicians were making sure the helos cranked and that all major and backup navigational systems were working smoothly.

At the same time an AC-130H Spectre gunship was being readied in one of the airstrip's hangars. Spooky— as the AC-130H was fondly nicknamed—had the range and the firepower to take down security threats to the team's extraction, and also to protect the heavy lifters as they made a run for the Persian Gulf across the lower half of Iran with the Mean One onboard.

Now, as the team began to cross the flat expanse of the open desert, the Marines started noticing broken lines of craters covering the landscape. Saxon recognized these land features. They were holes in the earth created by the subsidence of the desert crust into a cavern system running beneath the ground.

The northern deserts of the Middle East were once submerged beneath a prehistoric ocean that shrank back to create the Caspian Sea to the northeast, the Mediterranean to the west and the Persian Gulf to the south, as well as numerous rivers and lakes in between.

It wasn't just oil that flowed underneath the desert, it was water too. It flowed in rivers and pooled in huge cisterns trapped in sandstone aquifers. The team was probably crossing a cavern system through which one such underground river flowed, emptying into the Gulf via caves on the distant coast beyond the Zagros range.

Before long, the unpredictable weather again turned sour on the unit. It was at 0130 hours, in the midst of a sudden *shamal*, that one of Saxon's reconnaissance patrols reported in with an alert.

"Boss, we got some Girl Scouts coming on bearing Hotel Bravo-Niner. I make it a motorized company. Couple of Bimps and a truck full of raghead crunchies. They've picked up our trail, no doubt of it."

"That's a roger," Saxon said back. "Maintain visual contact. Report back every ten."

"I copy that. On it."

Saxon keyed off his comms.

A little later, Saxon got another message from his scouts.

"Boss, they've halted. Something's up. I don't know what yet, though."

"Keep scoping them out. When you get a handle on what they're up to, get on the horn."

"Yessir."

About five minutes passed, and then the team's pucker-factor skyrocketed. Aircraft were again heard vectoring in. The sounds were different this time. It wasn't the rotor noises of smaller choppers—the black gunships that had hit and chased them before—they now heard. It was a single heavy lifter, sweeping in at higher altitude. Something about this made Saxon especially alert, though he couldn't say exactly why. There was just a foreboding that something was wrong. Real wrong. A minute later, Saxon learned he'd been more than merely paranoid.

"Boss, it's a Harke that's coming and if my eyes don't deceive me there's a daisy cutter hanging off the bottom."

"Say again."

"A daisy cutter, Boss. A BLU-82 complete with U.S. markings. No shit."

"Damn, I knew some shit was about to go down."

Yeah, Saxon thought. It was possible. This was Iran. There were tons of weapons left over from the Shah's reign and Ollie North's chickenshit guns-for-hostage dealing in the mid-eighties, stuff that even survived eight years of meatgrinder warfare with Iraq. Yeah, it was possible, all right.

Saxon issued immediate instructions to his patrols and then to the rest of the detachment over the secure radio net. He ordered the unit to grab as much gear, ammo and weapons as possible and leave the vehicles behind. They were to rappel down into the craters in the desert crust and take cover in the subterranean cavern system on the double.

Vehicle doors slammed, bootleather beat ground, men shouted and cursed as they unfurled ropes and hastily unshipped rappelling gear, scrambling to evacuate the surface before all hell broke loose. It all took minutes and felt like hours, but by the time the Harke came thundering overhead, beating the air with its huge main rotors, the last Marine was grabbing his helmet and biting the dirt on the hard cavern floor.

High overhead, some bad shit indeed was about to happen.

The ton-and-a-half worth of fuel-air explosive—a conventional bomb the size of a Volkswagen Beetle—was cut loose from the helo at the top of the aircraft's flight ceiling. It plunged to earth, detonating about sixty feet above ground, subjecting a football stadium–sized area to an airburst and firestorm rivaled only by a subkiloton nuclear blast.

Forty feet underground, the caverns in which the Marines had taken refuge shook, and portions of the cavern ceiling gave way, burying soldiers alive under tons of fallen debris. Above, at ground zero, the detachment's Hummers were completely incinerated and the missiles and ammo stores left behind cooked off in the midst of the larger inferno. Gouts of fire whooshed down into the craters like the flaming breath of dragons, searching for human prey. More casualties were taken as men too close to the crater shafts were badly burned. All of them were shaken up like flies in a matchbox as the ferocious onslaught pounded with all its might against the cavern roof.

When the tremors subsided, Saxon gathered the stunned survivors together, shouting and slapping reality back into those who were too dazed to function. His men needed their wits about them, and fast. Saxon feared that the opposition force—and he was not entirely certain of its identity at this point—might send in combat troops after dropping the hammer on them.

Which is exactly how it went down.

Commando forces were soon fast-roping from transport helos and rappelling into the cavern system after their blast-shocked quarry. It was a platoon-strength contingent, armed with AK-class automatic rifles and the light, box-fed machine guns called squad automatic weapons by infantry soldiers.

The attackers had the advantage of shock and surprise in their favor and they had fallen on a force still dazed from the effects of the walloping bomb strike. The shock tactics were effective and in the first few seconds of the assault the invaders took still more casualties among Saxon's beleaguered troops. But the Marines soon rallied and their rage at the enemy drove away every other concern. Saxon's troops hit back with savage counterattacks that first blunted the assault and then turned the tide of battle. In the brief but bloody underground battle, the Marines steadily whittled down the assault forces to a stub, shooting and grenading most of the enemy and bayoneting the rest until the cavern floor ran with blood and the air of the tunnels was close with the stench of cordite and death.

When the hellaceous firefight was over, Saxon examined the unfriendly KIAs. They wore Iranian regular army battle dress and carried natively manufactured AK variants. The enemy was now a known quantity. They had been attacked by Iranian forces, not paramilitary black operatives out of Incirlik. This meant that they had either evaded the scalpel teams or that the dogs had been finally called off. The distinction was hardly a cause for celebration—dead was dead, no matter who killed you.

And now Marine Force One had to find a way to its extraction zone without motorized transport and most of its ammo and food stores. One still had its radios and GPS gear, but even if these continued to function, they weren't reliable deep underground. A safe exit from the cavern system would need to be found without benefit of sophisticated positioning devices.

Stripping their dead of dog-tags, burying friendly KIAs beneath cairns of stones, and bandaging the wounded, the MF-1 detachment now navigated the cavern system by magnetic compass and NVG-enhanced visual reconnaissance. The idea was to keep due east, in the direction of the planned extraction site at Masiriyah.

The notion of following the underground river down to the coast, suggested by Sgt. Hormones, was nixed by Saxon who pointed out that at least fifty miles of hard going lay ahead. Even if they made it to the Gulf coast, it was doubtful a seaborne extraction from there was doable. No, the team would stick to the original extraction plan and try to carry it out. That was their best, and probably their only, shot.

Hours later, after a forced march with only a single rest break, the Marines came to another rock chimney that led up onto the floor of the desert.

Saxon sent a five-man recon squad roping up the chimney to scout the perimeter and determine whether it was secure or not. Once topside on the desert crust, night-seeing binoculars were brought into play and the squad scanned the four compass points for signs of unfriendlies in the vicinity.

But there was nothing amiss out in the desert night. All around them was a flat, sere landscape broken only by massive sandstone pillars that jutted up here and there like the pegs of broken teeth in a giant's mouth. The squad leader was about to stow his field glasses and report back to Saxon when he saw the constellation of tiny, yellow stars; fairy lights that shimmered and danced on the horizon line as they passed between the pillars.

Sergeant Hormones continued to train his field glasses on the fairy lights, studied the spectacle awhile, nodded to himself in confirmation at what he'd surmised, then climbed down to report.

"Boss, the coast is clear. There's a road or highway about five klicks due east. I saw the headlights of some cars or maybe trucks heading south just before."

Saxon ordered Jeckyll up top with Hormone's scouts. Jeckyll was to set up his computer rig and GPS equipment and do a fast map recon to pinpoint their position. A security detail armed with SAWs and SMAWs was also sent topside onto the flat desert crust.

Saxon decided to climb up and eyeball the scene for himself, ordering the main force to fall out below. After breathing the stink of death for hours it was good to feel

the bite of the chill night wind against his face and inhale
the cold, fresh desert air. In the distance, more dancing
pinpoints suddenly sprang into being, then just as quickly
disappeared.

Yeah, there was a road there, all right.

Jeckyll had by this time set up his rig and performed a
preliminary map recon.

"Boss, we're about forty klicks southeast of our last
position," he reported. "The road we've seen is called
Highway Seven, which runs between Tehran and a place
called Chah Rabat at the mouth of the Gulf of Oman."

"What's our position relative to Masariyah?" Saxon
next asked.

Jeckyll told him that they were less than thirty klicks
away from the hoped-for extraction site.

Saxon nodded and told Jeckyll to try and raise the rescue team over satcom. This turned out to be a tougher bill
to fill because the equipment was still not working right.

Finally Jeckyll managed to connect to Eisenhower, the
Nimitz-class carrier anchored off the Omani coast that
was coordinating the extraction effort. A complicated arrangement followed by which the team communicated
through three parties with the chopper rescue detachment
gearing up to go from Misery Island.

After the palaver over the airwaves, Saxon realized that
the unit could still reach the extraction site at Masiriyah,
at least in theory. It would be a little later than originally
planned, because they'd lost all their motorized transport
and had been forced to stage a fighting withdrawal.

But Saxon figured that with luck maybe some new
transport might be picked up on the highway. If One could
commandeer itself some trucks, that could change the
time-frame completely.

Saxon issued orders for the rest of the team to climb

out of the hole in the earth and form up by squad. The
Mean One's Marines were to march toward Highway
Seven and deploy along its flanks. He would tell them
what to do next when they got there.

chapter *thirteen*

From here to a vanishing point in the north between the rock-ribbed ramparts of the Zagros mountains, the highway stretched ruler-straight, paralleling the easternmost bifurcation of the coastal mountain range right up to the Turkish border. In fact, Jeckyll's map recon made clear that the highway was part of the Bonn to Karachi truck route that Saxon's crew had begun to investigate back in the Swiss Alps several weeks before.

Along this route traveled the trucks that had departed from Germany toward Pakistan, carrying contraband dual-use technology destined for the new Soviet Union. And, going in the other direction, the Soviets were using the selfsame route to shuttle military gear into Iraq to complement the clandestine air cargo flights across the Elburz and northern Iran to Iraqi installations beyond the border.

But more surprises were to come. As Saxon and the team scouted out the highway, they saw, around a distant bend, the procession of wheeling, flickering starpoints that marked several pairs of approaching headlights. Saxon watched the headlights appear and disappear as the road looped around the colossal sandstone pillars that rose for several miles along its flanks. As he watched, a lightbulb flashed on in his head.

"Hirsh, you thinking what I'm thinking?"

"About dem trucks?"

"Yeah."

"I t'ink we both got the same idea."

"Switzerland."

"I gotcha."

"Jeckyll," Saxon next said, turning to his main technical. "Do a fast computation on travel time between here and Frankfurt for that truck convoy we saw leave. See if it's possible that it's the same one."

"On it."

Jeckyll entered data into the PC and in a couple of minutes came back with the answer.

"Affirmative," he replied. "Allowing for downtime on the road that could definitely be the same convoy. Pretty neat if we hitch ourselves a ride on those trucks, huh?"

"You know it," Saxon replied, and ordered the rest of the unit to get their heinies in motion. The team needed to deploy along the flanks of the road and be ready to interdict the convoy. In order to do that it would need to be in position well in advance of its approach.

The team reached the road while the convoy was still at least a mile away. It was rolling on, doing about thirty miles on the road, moving at a steady pace down the highway.

Saxon ordered Sgts. Mainline and Berlin' Hirsh to set up fire positions with SMAW rockets, and Chicken Wire to get ready with his M-60E3 "Pig" GPMG. On his signal they were to launch rocket salvos and small arms fire at either side of the road, though placing their strikes wide enough to make sure the blacktop stayed undamaged.

If the lead truck—or any of the others behind it—ignored the warning salvos and tried to barrel their way through the blockade, Hirsh was to open up and shoot the driver of the lead vehicle.

The ambush went down pretty much as Saxon had anticipated. The salvo of SMAW rocket strikes did its work, and the lead truck stopped short, its hood thrown back against the windshield and its shattered engine block gushing flames and dense black smoke. The other trucks behind it followed suit with barely enough clearance to keep from slamming into each other as their drivers stomped on their brakes.

The men in the truck cabs saw the night begin to swarm with armed commandos and came out with their hands up, doing exactly as ordered. For the truckers, the road to Karachi had just dead-ended. The convoy was now in 1-Patcher hands.

Saxon set his people to checking out the captured trucks before they were commandeered as transport. Inside their cargo areas, most of the rigs were loaded with weaponry, heavy machinery, spare parts and miscellaneous components. Saxon ordered everything videotaped for the intel people back at the Pentagon and Langley to whack off over, and then had two of the trucks cleaned out.

One wasn't very full and posed little problem. The remaining three were packed to the bursting and the other two had to be laboriously emptied by means of back-breaking grunt work. The final truck was driven off the road and blown up with a missile strike.

As to the drivers, Saxon ordered them blindfolded, gagged, tied up and left near the wreckage with some food and water nearby. It would take them a while to work themselves loose, and by that time it wouldn't make much difference to the Mean One whether they provided directions to pursuers or not.

Saxon's crews climbed aboard their new transport, again making for their planned extraction site. They drove through the night and into the gloaming of early morning. At the same time as this was happening, the Sea Stallions and their AC-130H Spectre escort had already launched from Misery Island and were en route across southern Iran to the pickup site.

The aircraft weaved a stomach-turning, swooping, diving course through the coastal mountains, following a path that stitched them through the invisible holes in overlapping ground radar coverage like a thread being passed through the eyes of a dozen scattered needles.

The choppers and Spooky began their penetration of Iranian airspace at four hundred feet, but as they moved inland and crossed the canyons and rift valleys between the coastal mountains, they averaged an altitude of as low as twenty feet above ground.

As they flew nap of the earth, their flight paths controlled by terrain-following guidance systems, the aircraft zigged and zagged, twisting and turning to keep their fuselages hidden amid the ground clutter, but also lurching and swaying in crosswinds and thermals that buffeted the aircraft and complicated the already difficult maneuvers.

There was as much seat-of-the-pants flying here as flying on instruments, and the reactions, skill and daring of pilots were just as important to the successful inbound flight as the high-technology navigational aids the aircraft used to make the incursion.

At last, after over an hour of these gut-wrenching aerobatics, the three aircraft cleared the main spine of the mountains and overflew the far lower foothills that extended for several score miles from their base.

The aircrew now knew that there would not be much more flight time left. They had almost reached their destination and the radio direction finder pod mounted just beneath the AC-130H's left cockpit windshield was already picking up coded signals from the Marines' transponder beacon.

Marine Force One had made the abandoned salt mine without further incident and fanned out into defensive positions. The cargo trucks were parked just within the walls of the huge open pit, at the end of a sloping access road, and so positioned as to be available for cover in case unfriendlies appeared. This turned out to be a prudent precaution, because an assault was not long in materializing.

Suddenly the air was split by missile strikes as an armored enemy force appeared on the perimeter of the mine. As the Marines returned fire, Saxon had Jeckyll radio for an ETA on the airborne extraction package.

Jeckyll reported that the rescue mission was currently fifteen minutes away from their position. Jeckyll also notified the inbound aircrews that it would be a hot extraction, as they were now under heavy attack. Spooky affirmed that report and took the lead, outdistancing the choppers to give cover fire for the rescue force.

The AC-130H Spectre gunship arrived on scene to find the Mean One facing a regiment-sized ground force of Iranian regular troops as well as an airborne squadron of attack helicopters. Spooky's FCO or fire control officer, usually irreverently abbreviated as "Fucko," ordered his crew to go in after the helos first, and the Spectre's gunners opened up on the attack choppers with front-mounted 20 mike-mike Vulcan cannon fire and the 105 mike-mike automatic howitzer that was mounted in the well just behind the left wing. A flaming hail of the thirty-two-pound projectiles fired by the howitzer slammed into the enemy choppers, literally ripping them apart in midair.

Spooky next went after the enemy ground troops. It began pouring fire down at the Iranians while One emptied its guns at the bearded men in olive drab opposing them on the ground. Between the AC-130H and One the Iranian regiment was quickly whittled down to a bloody butt-end. The remnants of the force soon withdrew to sheltered fire positions while their commander radioed for reinforcements.

Amid continuous firing, and before fresh troops could arrive on the scene, the two CH-53E Sea Stallions landed inside the abandoned salt mine. With engines idling they began taking on evacuees.

With full loads of grateful Marines, the choppers rose up off the ground and began the outbound leg of their flight. They were thousands of pounds heavier by now, and their fuel stores were borderline, but each CH-53E was certified to carry a nine-ton payload and each Stallion had been outfitted with two external 450 gallon drop tanks, enough to nearly double its five-hundred mile range. The AC-130H continued to ride shotgun as the mission made a run back to the Iranian coast.

* * *

Onboard the helos, Marine Force One was dazed and confused. Some of the men experienced the post-battle euphoria that can overcome soldiers after prolonged combat. Under the circumstances this was a dangerous high to ride. There were still almost two hours of flight time left, involving tricky negotiation of miles of treacherous terrain. The mission was still open to attack by Iranian aircraft.

In short, they were all still in the shit and had no cause to party.

"Fighters," the lead helo pilot suddenly announced.

The euphoria died as quickly as it had come on.

Dead ahead there were MiG-29 Fulcrums. Two first-line fighters manned by Iran's best pilots. The fighters closed in, going after the AC-130H Spectre first, which they rightfully judged to be their most serious threat. Spooky had a fight on its hands, and its flight crew all knew it. While the pilot kept the left wing-tip pointed at the oncoming planes, the Fucko's sensor operators locked on with their radar and infra-red target identification and acquisition systems, awaiting their chief's order to commence firing. The Fucko gave the order and Spooky's 20 mike-mike Vulcan gun array, 40 mike-mike cannon and 105 mike-mike howitzer unleashed a coordinated pattern of fire at the incoming fighters.

The trick here was to get the planes on the first salvo, because the AC-130H Spectre was not an aircraft designed for aerial combat. Intended to take on ground targets, all the plane's guns and most of its sensors were located on the left side of the fuselage, and an attack on its vulnerable blind side could easily prove fatal.

Spooky's crew cheered as they saw one of the MiGs

take a hit and go spinning out of control, its right wing completely chewed off by a burst of intense automatic and cannon fire. More of the fighter fuselage disintegrated under the steady barrage, and the burning, smoking hulk went spinning out of control, the shot-up pilot ejecting in a bloody, burning mass and falling to earth without his chute ever opening.

The rest of the smoke-spewing metal eggshell went smashing into the side of a mountain, exploding into a balloon of fire and scattering blast debris down the sheer slope to the floor of the canyon below.

The second Fulcrum had been hit by Spooky's fire too, but it managed to evade mortal damage and returned fire at the AC-130H while winging-over onto the Spectre's blind-side. A salvo of AA-11 missiles exploded near the gunship and jagged, whirling shrapnel tore into the skin of the nacelle of its right prop engine.

With one engine now dead, the AC-130H went into a spin. Before the pilot could compensate, Spooky had crashed into the cavern wall and burst into flames, and the airframe's wreckage cascaded to the rock floor below.

With the Spectre gone the surviving MiG came hurtling after the Stallions. By this time, though, pursuer and pursued alike had flown into the teeth of another cyclonic sandstorm. With visibility cut down by the *shamal*, infrared and radar targeting accuracy was reduced, and the choppers evaded missile strikes that slammed into the mountainside, sending gouts of shattered rubble spraying against their rotors and hulls. The lone MiG tried to follow but was leaking hydraulics by now. Its manual backup flight control systems had begun to fail too. Spooky hadn't killed the Fulcrum outright, but it had injected slow poison into its veins that would end up killing it by delayed reaction.

With the top of the canyon wall looming up in front of his cockpit, the Fulcrum pilot tried one last time to pull up his plane's nose, but it was like stirring a kettle of mush with his joystick and he knew he'd never make it in the second or two he had left.

A split-second after he yanked the ejection lever, the nose of the Fulcrum struck the side of the canyon, and the plane flipped back on its belly like a hooked marlin, crashing upside down into the reverse slope of the canyon. A massive fireball marked the spot where it exploded into a thousand fragments.

A few hundred feet slant-range of the crash, the pilot's chute opened and he floated to earth unconscious, never feeling the harsh impact with the ground that broke his collarbone in three places until he came to, much later, to find himself alone in a bleak and savage place.

The two Sea Stallions reached the Gulf coast over an hour later. Their auxiliary drop tanks had been sucked dry and jettisoned not long after dustoff, and their main tanks were now almost out of fuel. In addition, one of the choppers had been damaged by munitions strikes during the fight with the MiGs. The lead chopper made it in for a landing on Masirah island, but the second helo, its right GE turboshaft engine now noticeably trailing a plume of sooty black smoke, was forced to ditch in the sea.

Saxon was among those onboard who had to bail out and swim for the rescue boats that were sent out from the Eisenhower's support ships. As he dog-paddled to safety he heard a familiar voice shout a familiar refrain.

"Lord, how I just fucking luvvvvv the Marines," Sgt. Mainline was bellowing as he stroked toward the boats. Saxon almost believed him.

book three

*You Don't Hurt 'Em
If You Don't Hit 'Em*

chapter *fourteen*

Like any true carrion-eaters the White House press corps knew when something rank was in the wind.

In the space of forty minutes three official limos, each bearing the flag of the SecDef, the CJCS and State, respectively, were seen rolling through the gates of the West Wing entrance. Wireless palmtops and cell phones were instantly in hands and pressed against ears.

Some reporters continued to stand vigil outside the White House, phoning in reports or sending e-mails to their respective White House newsdesks.

Others, phones pasted to ears, pens scribbling on touch-sensitive screens, hastened to the White House press room, where they hoped to find explanations for the VIP arrivals and find a seat for the press briefing they suspected was imminent. At the very least, Percy Higgins, the White House press secretary, could be relied on for some immediate off-the-record quotes on whatever the developing situation might involve.

Suddenly one of the newsmedia people who were crowding the West Wing entrance gate was heard to shout to his assistant that the chairman of the Joint Chiefs was seen getting out of his limo carrying a number of charts and audiovisual aids.

A buzz immediately spread through the gathered journalistic throng. Those who had put away their cell phones and wireless gadgets brought them out again.

Others who had been en route to the press room stopped in their tracks and fed more information to their headquarters. The sighting of the maps was significant. It always signaled that an important briefing would soon be taking place in the Oval Office.

The chairman of the Joint Chiefs, General Buck Starkweather, was a green-suiter. No matter that the Pentagon's chiefs of staff were supposed to mentally clothe themselves in nonpartisan purple—a mixture of Army green and Air Force and Navy blue—the service chiefs could never escape the imperatives of service or the dictates of career.

Starkweather had arrived at the White House not very long after one of the regular morning meetings of the chiefs, this one held in the SecDef's third-floor E-ring office. While the chiefs do convene in the Tank for briefings, this famous Pentagon conference room is not by any means their sole place to discuss military affairs.

The chiefs have considerable latitude in where, when and how they will meet, and often convene at different places in the Pentagon at different times, and for different purposes. During times of intense crisis, a secure conference room overlooking the operations pit in the National Military Command Center might be utilized, for example.

For highly secret discussions the Tank, which is kept ultra-secure against electronic eavesdropping, might be used, but there are also various other sterile rooms available in the depths of the Pentagon that are far more secure than even the Tank or the NMCC's conference suite.

For most occasions, though, the private office of the Secretary of Defense is the meeting place of choice. Apart from other considerations, the SecDef's office is spacious and is located adjacent to a small but extremely well-stocked kitchen from which hot food, canapés, fresh-brewed coffee and other delicacies are always served to the chiefs.

The bottom line is that the U.S. Defense Secretary is the boss of the Pentagon. The Building is the house over which he presides. Some SecDefs prefer to delegate functions to subordinates. Some, like the present one, do not, and so Lyle Dalhousie, wingtip Oxford-shod feet perched across the immense Pershing desk that had been a fixture of the third-floor office since the end of World War I, presided over yet another morning meeting of the chiefs.

Although this morning's main topic of discussion continued to be the war in the Balkans, a new situation of growing concern was where the Soviets might be moving next. The Soviets had begun to pull back from Bulgaria and the Romanian border, and Russian-backed insurgency into Kosovo and Macedonia in the former Yugoslavia had begun to evaporate.

The peace treaty that had been brokered by the UN at the Helsinki peace summit a few weeks before was being honored, and UN peacekeeping forces were monitoring the phased withdrawal of NATO and Warsaw Pact troops from the Balkan theater. Despite these positive signs, the mood was tense. The Bear was still in a very belligerent mood, and he was beginning to turn in a new direction, scenting the wind and baring his teeth.

The chiefs, their deputies, and their civilian counterparts at Defense closed the meeting with a consensus opinion that would be brought before the president later on that day. General Starkweather, armed with his charts, now began to relay that consensus to his commander in chief.

"**G**entlemen . . . Mr. President," Starkweather began. "These digital images you now see on the screen represent an intelligence coup of the first magnitude. They came from an elite Marine Corps special operations unit that has recently returned from a mission in the Middle East.

"Operation Speedball was intended to both conclusively establish the nature of armament shipped to Iraq and to interdict the clandestine channels of supply between Moscow and Baghdad. The operation, conducted jointly by the CIA and the Pentagon, involved the insertion of a special unit into the Elburz mountain region bridging the northern borders of Turkey and Iran. The Russians were using the high mountain passes to transport planeloads of matériel to the Iraqis."

The CJCS clicked his wireless remote and satellite photos of the Elburz region flashed across the screen. Taken from orbital space by multimillion-dollar camera-eyes, they were of crystal-sharp resolution. The mountain pass that the Mean One had staked out was clearly recognizable within a blue circle that drew the eye toward it.

"In this complex operation, our forces were able to get inside one of the transport planes in order to document and analyze the cargo it carried."

The CJCS clicked again, and again. Imagery of the cargo of the Antonov gathered by MF-1 filled the screen.

"Here, in these frames, we can pick out some of the weapons components that have been in the process of reaching sites inside Iraq. There are several, but I want to draw your attention to these specifically . . ."

Again the remote clicked, and clicked again. Starkweather got out a laser pen and directed the red pinpoint beam at the image of the contents of one of several long crates that had been lashed to the Antonov's deck.

"These are artillery tubes, Mr. President. Not ordinary artillery tubes, by any means, however. Such tubes are for super-howitzers, monsters with a three-hundred-thirty-millimeter bore that we know the Russians have been developing along the lines of one of the prototypes of the infamous Bull supergun.

"You can see the strategic implications on this next map. The increased artillery range it gives Iraq would enable it to possess the equivalent of accurate ballistic missiles at a small fraction of the cost. From inside the borders of Iraq their batteries could then hit targets in Syria, Jordan, even Turkey or Iran."

The president knew about the superguns from previous intelligence reports, but the graphic detail of the CJCS's presentation brought the dangerous implications of this development home to him in a very powerful way.

"I'm told we can hit many of the installations these guns have already been set up at, but not all of them."

"Correct, Mr. President," the CJCS went on. "Not all of them. And even one surviving installation poses a global danger. Those others are in hardened installations. Deep underground facilities or DUFs. We can damage those DUFs with conventional cruise missile strikes, but only direct nuclear intervention can destroy them using standoff weapons."

"Can't do it. No nukes. At least none we're forced to admit having used. It has to stay covert. And I'm assuming that the small nuclear blasts we can hide won't do the trick."

"Correct, sir. But I wasn't suggesting we exercise our white-world nuclear option, Mr. President."

"Then what did you mean, Bucky?"

"A force on the ground, sir. A trained force of special operators. A sizeable force, perhaps multinational in scope. A regional force under the control of a U.S. commanding officer stationed in the area. If you will, Mr. President, you may think of it as a special forces or covert version of the Desert Storm coalition of 1991."

The president leaned forward, clearly interested. The CJCS had just set the gears in his politically attuned mind turning. Here was a concept that might resonate with Congress and the voters alike.

"Go on, General," the president advised Starkweather. "You got me interested."

"Well, sir. What we have in mind is based on the urgent need to put a big cancellation mark on Saddam Hussein's still nascent but developing capability to set up those superguns and fire advanced hybrid artillery shells in a new bid for regional dominance. The shells are part conventional projectile, part guided missile, and they have so-called clip-on capability—"

"What the hell's that again, Buck?"

"That, Mr. President, means they can be easily refitted with unconventional warheads, such as nuclear, biological or chemical armament. Conventional warhead modules are basically removed by technicians and the unconventional modules installed. The system is fully modular. The advanced projectiles can be very rapidly converted."

"Shee-yitt."

"That's absolutely right, Mr. President," the CJCS went on. "And plenty of it, unless we do something. We know Saddam has a few of the superguns already set up in fixed and mobile launch sites. We don't think he has the exotic, or unconventional warhead clip-ons yet, or only enough to run tests on. We want to stop him cold before that happens. And that means destroying his capability on the ground.

"What about our Soviet friends?"

"We think the Russians will see that backing off on this one will be the better part of valor. We've left them pretty much with a free hand in the Caucasus, which was their main objective in starting the war anyway. The Mideast is basically a sideshow to the homeboys at Two Dzerzhinsky Square. We think they'll back off."

"OK. Go on."

"Mr. President, for the rest, I believe Marine Commandant Clifford should continue. It's his people who will be leading the charge."

Clifford took the floor.

"The multinational brigades will be led by Marine Force One, the Marine Corps' new special forces unit. We are at this stage calling the initiative Operation Sand Viper. Here is what we have in mind . . ."

The president was listening. He liked the name Sand Viper. It had media appeal. He could probably even sell it to the house majority on the other side of the aisle. On the legal pad in front of him, he doodled a picture of a snake biting a mustachioed man on the backside while, with the trace of a smile, he listened to the rest of what the Marine commandant had to say.

"Oh, and one more thing I should mention, Mr. President," Clifford went on with studied casualness, unclipping a laser pen from his tunic pocket.

"Yes, General. What's that?"

"We think it's possible the Iraqis may have something even bigger than those three-hundred-thirty-millimeter tubes stashed away"—he pointed with the laser beam to a spot on a map that an aide had just set up on an easel—"Right here."

The president suddenly stopped doodling. He wasn't smiling anymore either.

A few thousand miles and several time zones away, the U.S. president's Soviet counterpart sat pondering matters of similar importance. The Soviet premier's *poputchik* was behaving just as planned. The swaggering puppet was eager to absorb as much Russian weaponry and manpower as he could.

All in all, it was a display on an even grander scale than the Russian incursion into Egypt under Nasser in the late fifties, which lasted until the late sixties and the ascendancy of Sadat. Starchinov's predecessors in the Kremlin hierarchy had then sought to arm Egypt as a counterbalance to the West's sphere of influence in Iraq.

In those days, at the start of the Cold War, it was Baghdad that was the most pro-Western of the Arab states, and Egypt that was seen to be slipping from the American-led alliance. Today, of course, the opposite situation prevailed. For decades Egypt had, absent Israel, been the most powerful Western surrogate in the region, whereas Iraq had become a pariah state. So it went, in a dialectic swing that Karl Marx had seen and described long ago.

Now it was Iraq's turn to swallow the Soviet bait. So far, Starchinov's *poputchik* was hungry for as much of it as he could have. The premier's last reports told of secret junkets on the Illyushin mini-jet the Kremlin had supplied, one that had been bugged with sensitive yet undetectable listening devices that beamed to a Soviet orbital listening post virtually everything said by the Iraqi autocrat to his trusted aides.

However, the Kremlin leader also knew that the West had detected these new inroads into Iraq and would take steps to counter them. It was, of course, inevitable that they would, and in the political sphere there was little if anything they could do about it.

The military sphere posed a separate set of challenges where an entirely different array of rules applied. Just as the Western alliances had waged a covert war against Nasser in the old days, so they were already showing signs of doing this today against his own strategic maneuverings.

Starchinov would have to counter these countermoves. At the least he would need to stage holding actions until completion of the deep installations that Soviet technicians and construction crews were already busily digging in the Iraqi deserts to house the new superguns that the *poputchik* of Iraq was acquiring.

After these preparations were finished, it would be too late for the U.S. and her allies to do anything about it. They would never use thermonuclear weapons on first-strike terms, which was the only effective means to destroy the underground bases. Nor could they use small, subkiloton "tinynukes" on such an objective either. They were extremely limited, little better than conventionals.

The geo-strategic implications were strikingly clear to Starchinov. It was a game of dominoes. His *poputchik* would strike the West's *poputchik* states, which included those, like Syria or Jordan, that claimed nonalignment.

Once they were destroyed or had capitulated, it would be
the Persian giant's turn to feel the lash. Apart from control
of vital oil reserves, the threat posed by the Islamist and
ethnic rebels in Iran would be quelled. Russia would
emerge stronger than before, a true superpower once
again.

Then it could press outward, along its northeastern
flanks. Once the borders to the south were sealed, those
on the Baltic would fall between the crosshairs. And after
these were brought back into the Soviet orbit as satellites . . .

An aide interrupted the premier's apocalyptic musings.
Important visitors from the intelligence services and GRU
had just arrived. They were to advise Starchinov of breaking developments in the Mideast.

Starchinov gave instructions to permit them entry, then
positioned himself at his desk, looking downward. When
they entered he would make them wait for long minutes
while he appeared to busy himself with paperwork. It was
a technique that had worked well for Stalin, and one that
the current Soviet leader had perfected to a theatrical art.

Northeastern Jordan was a cold stone's throw from nowhere. The hyperbole was a bodyguard for truth in
this case. Strictest secrecy prevailed in the establishment
and logistical considerations for the Sand Viper headquarters.

A joint staff comprised of a Western contingent of
American, British and French officers on the one hand,
and a Mideast contingent of Syrian, Israeli and Hashemite
Jordanian officers on the other, could only be brought together under the tightest security conditions imaginable.

The groundwork for Sand Viper had been laid during

and in the aftermath of the funeral of King Hussein of Jordan. As crowds in Amman lamented the death of the king, the Western nations and other Arab states had stood alert to challenges to the young King Abdullah's reign, especially from the direction of Baghdad.

At the same time, Abdullah, who was a career military officer, was seen to be receptive to the West, and secret protocols were established for military intervention if necessary. Abdullah well knew that his chief adversary was Saddam Hussein, who reigned with a dictator's iron fist over a country many times his country's size and not very distant.

And so secret bases were established in the desert against the day when Iraq might grow strong again and prepare to once more attack its neighbors. That day, it seemed, was dawning. Intelligence assessments of Saddam's growing might and the superior weaponry he was receiving from Soviet sources were made available to Abdullah. The young king recognized the significance immediately. Orders were given to make the bases available for immediate occupation.

Major David Saxon, leader of Marine Force One, under the command of General "Patient K." Kullimore arrived soon after the base was prepared. Along with him came a contingent of staff personnel. Saxon, who would command special operations field initiatives, would set up shop and participate in planning sessions.

Soon the rest of MF-1 would follow the advance cadre. To the American special operations team would fall the task of training and organizing the coalition of commando warriors who would wage a series of crippling ground strikes against the forces being built up by Saddam Hussein. Operation Sand Viper slowly uncoiled, but would soon bare its fangs.

chapter *fifteen*

Somewhere below them, as they flew above Wadi Ar'ar, some of the aircrew caught a glimpse of the lines of overhead communications cables, petroleum conduits and four-lane blacktop that ran northwest-southeast along the eastern Saudi Arabian border between Jordan and the Persian Gulf.

This was the Tapline Road, built by the major international oil companies in the 1950s to service their oil pipeline stretching from the Gulf to the Med and intersecting Jordan, Syria and Lebanon, where it terminated a few miles south of Beirut.

A few miles east of the Tapline, sand berms cut across the ochre desert, roughly and intermittently paralleling the highway for several miles. The berms, the rusting and sand-scoured wreckage of military vehicles destroyed some fifteen years before, and the numerous unmarked graves that none aboard the helos could see from even this low altitude, were all signposts marking the sortie's entrance into Iraq.

There were military outposts, border and road checkpoints, sun-baked villages and encampments of Bedouin nomads to be found here too. There were also the invisible Doppler waves of ground tracking radars and the radars of SAM sites, including Roland and SA-10 batteries, to contend with.

The sector of the Iraqi desert was remote from the more populated quarter closer to Baghdad, but the overflight still presented a great danger of discovery to the airborne mission.

Those that had planned the mission—those at Drop Forge, the forward operation center in Jordan, as well as those in a vaulted room within the labyrinth of the National Military Command Center at the Pentagon—were aware of the threats and had tried to level the playing field somewhat.

For weeks prior to the mission, the borderlands that Iraq shared with Jordan, Syria and Saudi Arabia became the focus of planned incursions by ground and airborne forces.

Planes and helicopters would dart across the border, electronically tickle Iraqi tripwire forces, and then dart back, having orders not to engage unless fired upon.

Ground radar and SAM sites underneath the no-fly-zone's umbrella were also baited in this way. Ferret aircraft, including the RC-135(X) Cobra Eye, subjected cross-border radar stations and military listening posts to a barrage of electronic warfare attacks.

The stage-managed confusion was the prelude to tonight's two-pronged mission. The Iraqi military, who were as sophisticated as any other Middle Eastern nation's, and more so than some, knew that something was in the offing, but they didn't know what, how or when it would hit.

As long as they were kept off-balance, the mission had a good chance of success. The confusion, exploited to the maximum, was crowned by cruise missile strikes against targets outside Baghdad, the flashes of which were visible on the horizon as the sortie out of Saudi stole across the enemy's homeland.

The aircrew flew its inbound course in three dimensions. It not only navigated by terrain features, but dodged and jinked and slipped between the unseen feelers of microwaves, exploiting the open seams where radar coverage failed to tightly overlap.

Like microscopic parasites weaving between the scales of a sleeping shark, the three helicopter gunships flew their treacherous inbound course, first making use of Wadi Ar'ar to keep their hulls beneath the level of the ground, and then changing altitude and direction across the open desert beyond the wadi.

The Marine Corps' AH-1W Whiskey Cobras were loaded for bear. The weapons complement included HARM anti-radar missiles, Redeye infra-red homing missiles, Hydra unguided rockets and a few thousand rounds of .50-caliber ammo for the nose cannons that were slaved to the head movements of their pilots, deadly swiveling drones that could spit automatic fire at hundreds of rounds a minute.

The AH-1Ws were the door-kicking force for Boogie and Balls, the force elements of the double-barreled attack. Like the nose of the camel in the old Bedouin fable, the helos would open the way for the considerably larger portions of the ungainly beast that was waiting to climb inside the tent and take it over, at least for a while.

Following the waypoints on their flight plan, the helos continued on their convoluted journey into Iraq and, approximately twenty minutes into their flight, encountered the first of their two objectives.

The SAM site lay about fifty miles from the Saudi border and about six miles from the desert airstrip that was the helo sortie's secondary objective of the night. The SAM site was a high-to-medium envelope threat, comprised as it was of SA-6 and SA-9 launchers and their search-track radars that were capable of engaging aircraft out to sixty thousand feet.

The SAM site—actually there were two of them, counting the Roland battery and revetmented "Shilka" ZSU–23–4 triple-A guns at the airstrip—posed a serious threat to the hump of the camel and had to be taken out first thing. One AH-1W gunship was deemed enough to do the job, with the second helo tasked with securing the airstrip and the third along for backup. And so it came to pass as the Whiskey Cobras neared the first mission objective.

At this stage in the mission, the attack choppers had been flying nap of the earth, or NOE, as opposed to the low-level and contour flight paths inbound to their targets. NOE was the safest way to fly, but it was also the slowest, so it was reserved for the most critical and dangerous stretches of the trip and for the final few seconds before reaching the engagement zone.

Now, only a short distance off the desert, the lead chopper executed the pop-up maneuver called unmasking, and sprang from under ten feet to an altitude of about thirty feet above ground. Below, the heavy vehicles that made up the launchers, radars, power supplies and transportation for the missile battery were visible to the aircrew in the greens and blacks of night vision head-up displays.

A human figure sprang into action, firing a Kalashnikov

variant as he ran toward one of the trucks, crying out a warning, but it was too late for him or anyone else on the ground. In an instant, HARM anti-radar missiles shot off the launch rails at either side of the AH-1W, slamming into the radar trucks and blowing them sky high in a thunderclap of flame.

Redeye strikes followed the HARM rounds off the launchers, taking out communications trucks and support vehicles, and blowing apart other Iraqi soldiers regardless of whether they were trying to hide or trying to fight.

As the AH-1W circled the target, the pilot brought its nose cannon into play, slaving it back and forth to spray white tracer fire into whatever happened to be left semi-intact in the zone of death and fire below, including soldiers trying to surrender with their hands raised in the air, these latter being blown limb from limb by the firepower directed against them.

Modern war and modern society has desensitized Americans to the full implications of what their weapons did to the things they struck. To the young Marines onboard the chopper, the Iraqis had about as much reality as Nintendo simulations.

The other two choppers had by this time passed on toward the main objective, reaching it only a few minutes later. The small desert airstrip lay vulnerable beneath the moonless, star-flecked sky. The runway was large enough to land a C-5B Galaxy—a plane dubbed "Fat Albert" by its crews—loaded to about one-third capacity.

The C-5—the hump of the camel—would be barreling in behind the gunships, but it would be full to capacity with men and matériel, including fuel bladders to re-tank the helos. Much of the weight would be reduced by LOREX-dropping the mechanized armor and heavy guns it carried, and then the transport would circle and land to debark the troops onboard.

First the airstrip had to be secured, and the second and third gunships were soon engaged in doing precisely this. The work went quicker because there were fewer targets to contend with here, and the battle—if you could call a turkey shoot a battle—was over almost as fast as it had begun. Their grim work now accomplished, the Whiskey Cobras hovered at a safe distance, giving the inbound Fat Albert a wide berth.

The giant strategic heavy-lift aircraft was minutes behind the gunship sortie, and soon the earsplitting roar of its four massive TF39-GE-1C turbofan engines (they are said to have the equivalent power of forty-eight railroad locomotives) began to churn up the night almost as physically as the growing cloud of exhaust-blown sand that was disturbed by its slipstream and wing vortexes spread through the crystal-clear desert air.

The C-5 came in low, its rear ramp already lowered, and parachutes began to blossom. One after another, palletted and cushioned Bradley APCs, HUMVEEs and crates of weapons, ammo and gear came popping out the back end of the enormous metal bird.

In a matter of minutes, the cargo load was down on the ground, close but well clear of the landing strip, and the C-5 was turning in the air to make a second pass for a landing. Passing through clouds of smoke and fire from the burning Iraqi vehicles that flanked the landing strip, the super-transport screamed as reverse-thrust buckets came down and friction brakes were applied to landing gear. Before it had rolled to a complete stop on nitrogen-filled tires, Marine Force One was hustling to ramp-off and get down to the job of unpacking its combat gear.

Minutes later, with the sounds of automotive engines

coming to life in the background, 1st Sgt. Berlin' Hirsh
was on secure SINCGARS communication to the final
element of the mission.

"We're on the ground, Boss," the NCO reported. "Semper Gumbi. We're good to go."

Many miles away, and approaching their common objective from a different angle, Major David Saxon affirmed the transmission and told the Marine Force One
team members onboard the C-130H-30 Hercules.

The smaller transport plane was coming in at a higher
altitude. The landing of the first element at the airstrip
was a signal that the assault on the largest and most difficult of the mission's twin objectives would soon commence.

Now it was the turn of the element onboard the Herky
Bird.

Within a matter of minutes, the C-130H-30 had reached
the drop zone for the HALO insertion that would send a
company of Marine special forces operators under
Saxon's command gliding on the wind toward their target
several miles inland.

The plan was fraught with risk, besides being somewhat
alien to Saxon, who was straight-leg infantry through and
through. The paratroop landing had to coincide with
Balls' main ground assault or Saxon's element would be
caught in a quagmire with no way out.

But neither Saxon nor the others tried to think very hard
about that as the stick of parachutists lined up behind the
jumpmaster and waited for his signal to take a walk into
space and hit the silk.

At about the same time as this was happening, the
second element of the coordinated assaults inside

Iraq had reached its first phase line. Boogie was a company-strength unit whose mission was to secure a smaller and less heavily fortified or defended objective than the first air-ground element, Balls, which had the job of taking control of one of Saddam Hussein's presidential palaces.

These so-called palaces were much more than castles on the desert, as the name might imply. Some of them were really small cities, complete with apartment blocks, villas leading onto artificial lakes with artificial pleasure islands in their midsts, housing for sizeable contingents of troops and SAM batteries to protect them from air strikes.

In addition to all this, Saddam's larger "palaces" showed just the tip of the proverbial iceberg aboveground. These also harbored extensive subterranean networks of bunkers, research labs, military command posts, motor pool areas and much else beneath the visible portion on the surface.

While Saddam's guests or members of the Iraqi dictator's extended family—most of the presidential palaces were rarely visited by the *Rais* himself—cavorted in the lake or indoor Olympic pools, or sipped cool drinks beneath imported shade trees, or even played golf on the eighteen-hole courses some of the palaces featured on their country club–like expanses, cadres of scientists might be at work in the underground portion of the palace developing who-knew-what diabolical weapon of mass destruction.

Saddam Hussein, who considered himself the reincarnation of the ancient Babylonian potentate Nebuchadnezzar, used this over-under scheme in virtually every weapons design facility that he'd built, and there were hundreds scattered throughout Iraq, each one of them engaged in a cellular manufacturing or research process that compartmentalized the individual cells.

Few besides the *Rais* himself possessed a working knowledge of the entire picture of Iraq's weapons development programs.

The same Iraqi strategy that had led to the rounding up of human shields against Gulf War air strikes, and that had filled the sleeping areas of the Taiwathuna milk factory with innocent Iraqis above a chemical weapons plant, divided the presidential palaces into heavens and hells reminiscent of the ancient kingdoms of light and darkness ruled by Marduk and Tiamat of ancient Mesopotamian legend.

Those in the heavenly realm disported above, while those in Abaddon slaved over infernal machinery in the fiend's workshop.

The presidential palace at As Salima was the objective of strike force Balls. It was a large palace as Saddam's palaces went, but the fact that it was more than just a glorified country club for the Iraqi elite had been indicated by Western underground remote sensing scans using spy satellites.

For years Iraq had built no underground facilities, aware that U.S. satellites possessed remote-sensing capabilities using thermal imaging, synthetic aperture radar imaging and magnetic anomaly detection. Then the Iraqis got more adept at *maskirovka*, or camouflage and concealment, and tunnel hardening techniques, and started digging bunkers again. But the NSA's hardware also got better, so that it was getting increasingly more difficult for Saddam to hide his bags of dirty tricks underground. For one thing, earthbound magnetic anomaly detection by space-based platforms had become more accurate, and projects using massive amounts of metal were impossible to hide.

The largest of the Soviet-supplied superguns might be buried beneath a false dome in the As Salima palace. It was believed that this gun could blast a projectile through the dome and into orbit, at least if the Soviets had supplied Iraq with artillery tubes following the original plan for the "Baby Babylon" Bull gun, as indicated by evidence found on the Antonov transports. This is why the main push was to take over As Salima. Remote, space-based sensing had also indicated the possibility of large-bore barrels of the smaller, but still formidable, three-hundred-thirty-millimeter tubes at a secondary installation. The OPPLAN included a provision for these to be assaulted as well.

Balls and Boogie were preparing to take down these two objectives. Boogie was a mechanized ground force driving light armored vehicles. Boogie would be landed close to its objective, a medium-sized research facility. Using man-portable rocket launchers and small arms fire, in addition to the weapons on its rolling armor, Boogie would storm the lightly fortified weapons research station, conducting a recon by fire. Boogie's operational plan called for support by two of the three Whiskey Cobra gunships that had shot up the SAM site and secured the landing strip several miles to the southwest.

All three Whiskey Cobras had refueled using portable fuel bladders dropped along with the other paletted cargo from the C-5B Galaxy's hold, and two of the attack helos had dusted off to fly toward Boogie's staging area. As Boogie reached its phase line, the helos were bird-dogging the team at a distance of about a kilometer, running a security operation in case of attack as Boogie rolled its armor toward its position near the installation that was its target.

The combined Marines special forces would seize their individual objectives, thoroughly search the sites for evidence of the supergun technology, and destroy in place any weapons found with special demolition charges.

As of 0300 hours, Lima, all strike units were well en route to their tactical objectives under the OPPLAN.

chapter *sixteen*

The stick of paratroops waltzed out the side of the plane into the darkness of a moonless desert night, their night vision preserved by the red lights that had softly illuminated the cabin of the C-130H-30.

The gear that had been lashed down in webbing against the bulkheads or balanced on the deck was now securely strapped to the backs, fronts, legs, arms, and in some cases, heads, of the Marines jumping out of the hold of the plane and free-falling through space.

Now that gear was secured against their bodies, clipped to MOLLE harnesses, and in the cases of grenades, combat knives and rifles taped into place so that gun barrels were pointing down on landing, blades stayed secure in their scabbards, and cotter pins didn't catch on external objects and come loose.

One after another the members of MF-1 cast their fates to the desert winds as they fell through the C-130's propwash and steeled their bodies for the sudden jerk of the chutes unfurling and opening. And one by one this happened. One airfoil parasail after another popped into being above the desert-camo-fatigued soldier below it, until the entire stick of paras was underway.

As the Hercules disappeared into the night, the airborne force began the first leg of its controlled, tapering descent, a descent that, if all proceeded according to plan, would land the Marines right in the heart of the As Salima presidential palace just as Balls' mechanized ground component—codenamed Gorilla—and its single dedicated AH-1W helo gunship were attacking from the outside.

If there were any major snags, if the timing was too far off the mark, or something unforeseen happened, there could be major trouble. But the team had its collective mind fixed on the objective. Nobody was thinking of failure. Saxon hadn't trained them to do that. To the Marines of Force One the word didn't exist.

The stick of MF-1 paratroops had no way of knowing about a conversation that had taken place several hours before inside a villa of a presidential palace distant by many miles from their current position. Had they been privy to the conversation, they might have felt differently about the chances of their mission's ultimate success. They might have had serious misgivings, to say the least.

The speaker was Qusay Hussein, the Iraqi president's eldest son, a man despised and feared by Iraqis second only to his father. Qusay, who enjoyed pulling the teeth from the mouths and nails from the fingers of those who had fallen out of favor with him, and was rumored to have personally clubbed an adversary to death, was sitting at one side of a comfortable sofa of black Milanese leather that, like most of the villa's furnishings, had been custom-designed to his specifications.

The sun setting over distant mountains cast a warm, red-gold glow across the room, lighting up the wall where a large flat-panel TV showed an Italian soccer match in progress.

Qusay sipped a sherry from a cut-crystal goblet and his guest caught the flash of gold from the band of the Rolex Oyster on his wrist. Qusay set the glass down and continued speaking. The guest of the son of Saddam, who had spent the most part of several months at a smaller and somewhat less sumptuously appointed villa within the palace grounds, sat in an easy chair facing his host. He did not drink, but instead smoked a filterless Turkish cigarette.

Dr. Jubaird Dalkimoni, terrorist bombardier supreme, inhaled the pungent smoke as he carefully listened to Qusay's words. It was important to pay close attention whenever one of Saddam's trusted associates addressed him; he had learned this during his stay as the Iraqi president's guest.

With Saddam himself—who Dalkimoni had spent almost an hour with on two separate occasions since his arrival in Baghdad—it was also important to think the right thoughts, or at least appear to be thinking the right thoughts.

Saddam could be charming or he could be brutal, or again, he could be something in between. But Saddam was always paranoid, no matter how he might act, and on top of this he was convinced he possessed the omniscient power to detect treachery in the hearts of men merely by looking them in the eyes.

If Saddam saw the wrong thing, that was all he needed. Saddam would issue an order and you would be taken away to meet your fate—sometimes even shot by the Iraqi president himself. Dalkimoni had been warned that the best way to act in Saddam's presence was to keep your mouth shut and say yes to everything he said.

Dalkimoni had found that this was equally good advice with Qusay, who had increasingly taken over Saddam's projects in recent years. So Dalkimoni listened attentively, smoking his cigarette while Qusay spoke.

"I envy you, Jubaird, I truly do," Qusay said, his eyes not on the bomb-maker but on the Italian soccer team on whom he had bet a million dollars to win against their German opponents. "Very soon your—"

Suddenly Qusay stopped speaking and stared at the screen. Then, with a curse, he flung his unfinished drink at the wall. An aide appeared and began wiping at the stain while Qusay punched a quick-dial button on a compact satcom phone he unclipped from his belt.

With pretended unconcern, Dalkimoni listened to Qusay berate someone on the other end of the line about how his team was losing, and on certain punishments that would await certain parties unless certain things were done immediately to drastically change certain events on the soccer field.

Almost instantly, time was called in mid-play. A few minutes later, play resumed, but this time it was Qusay's team that was winning. Dalkimoni heard Qusay promise someone a bonus, and then he put away the phone, his aide handing him a fresh drink before disappearing back into the woodwork.

Still intent on the TV screen, and without so much as once having glanced Dalkimoni's way, Qusay picked up where he had left off before the interruption.

"Your name shall be numbered among those mighty

heros of legend. You, Dalkimoni, hold the keys to the universe in your hands. For it is you who will shepherd the Winged Bulls to glory."

"Thank you," Dalkimoni replied. "Yes, it is truly an honor as you say it is."

"Have all the preparations been made? Is everything in order for your journey? There must be no mistakes, no slipups. Failure cannot be tolerated. You know this."

"There shall be none, Excellency," Dalkimoni replied. "All is in readiness. The Winged Bulls shall be unchained and permitted to take flight. The prophesy made many thousands of years before shall be fulfilled."

"Excellent. That is all I wanted to hear from you, Dalkimoni," Qusay said and turned back to the television. Dalkimoni saw that he was again caught up in the action of the soccer match and had already forgotten all about him. The bomb-maker stubbed out his cigarette in the ashtray on the end table by the side of the chair, rose and then left.

They had been talking about nuclear bombs.

Saxon's parasail detachment continued to glide toward its mission objective. Although still distant by the better part of a kilometer, their rate of descent had increased as their altitude dropped. Saxon, at the lead of the airborne shock force, checked his wrist chronometer, whose luminous dial showed him that his troops were meeting their timetable.

He decided to break EMCON to ask for a situation report from his ground commander. He would do it by burst transmission over the Defense Tactical Internet. The encrypted data packets would travel up to a satellite then bounce down again, and would produce a random pulse of noise to anybody listening.

Saxon used the wrist-top keypad linked by cable to the satcom phone nestled in a MOLLE pouch and encoded a message. It was addressed in conventional e-mail format to the operation's domain name: hirsh@operation_viper.mil. Minutes later the message was received and an answer flashed on the wrist-top's screen.

"Am in position. Good to go. Attack to commence at 4030 hours."

Saxon keyed back, "Affirm."

The strike was proceeding as planned. The timetable was being met. All operational elements were coming together. The Fat Lady was warming up her act.

Saxon's parafoil team now could see the muted lights of the presidential palace growing closer and brighter. Each descending sky trooper knew that final preparations for landing needed to be made.

Within minutes, the team got in close enough to clearly make out the guards in the towers surrounding the base and the missiles ready for launch at SAM batteries here and there on the grounds. They saw too the gleam of the artificial lake and the stands of plane trees along three sides of the vast estate's circumference.

Of course the guards below soon spotted the descending sky troopers as well, but the sighting had come too late to do the Iraqis much good. At this stage the Gorilla ground element with its helo air support had already initiated contact with the enemy. As Saxon's parasail team came dropping in for the kill, new sights and sounds overwhelmed the stillness of the night. They were the sounds of battle, the strobing flashes of rocket strikes and belch-

ing muzzle flames of automatic small arms fire. And in
the midst of it all, the sounds of men dying.

Barry White and Chaka Khan were fifteen minutes outbound from Jauf and cruising at eighty thousand feet.
At that altitude whether or not the search-and-track radars
of Iraqi SAMs painted them was immaterial.

They flew beyond the lethality envelope of all but the
very best SAMs Saddam fielded, and as far as these latter
went, they were at the very edge of their envelopes too.

But the chances of their being caught by radar were
slender at best. Both aircraft had radar cross sections as
small as the F-117A Nighthawk, but they were a hell of
a lot faster and more maneuverable than the stealth fighter.

The planes could afford to come in high, and it was
also tactically advantageous to do this. Coming in high
they would have a better chance of spotting any Iraqi
fighter assets that might be scrambled before the unfriendly planes saw them.

Then the Raptors would bare their claws.

Balls swept in toward its strike objective as Boogie
converged on the mission's secondary target. Codenamed Ripped, the complex at Al Athmidi was a medium-
sized installation that had recently been identified as
engaged in missile warhead and artillery projectile manufacturing. It also served as a storage entrepot for finished
product.

Being far smaller in size than the mission's primary
objective, the presidential palace at As Salima, the Al Athmidi installation was accorded a correspondingly smaller
take-down force. An assortment of low-rise cinderblock

buildings and Quonset huts was scattered across a bull-dozed stretch of desert about the size of two city blocks. This was Al Athmidi.

The facility was encircled by a twenty-foot-high hur-ricane fence generously topped by coils of razor wire. It was either manned by a detachment of specialist *Sai'qa* or Iraqi regulars; the intel was somewhat fuzzy on that score.

The troops had some heavy metal at the ready in case of attack, that much was clear—quad Shilka guns mounted on a BTR track chassis, sentries in two guard towers located to place intersecting fields of .50-caliber machine gun fire on approaching targets and maybe some smaller stuff too, such as Plamya automatic grenade launchers, known to be a favorite toy of Iraqi *Sai'qa* forces.

Saxon and MF-1's planning staff had proceeded on the assumption that the Iraqis had the surrounding desert di-vided into a grid system like the Germans had set up at Normandy, so spotters could radio in grid coordinates and the guard posts put fire on them without even needing visual contact with enemy forces.

The firepower at Al Athmidi was enough to pin down a medium-sized assault element, but Boogie packed enough firepower to overwhelm the base defenses, plus it would have the advantage of surprise in its favor.

Apart from the armaments on the Bradleys and HUM-VEEs, which included TOW missiles, the team was armed with Dragons—lighter-duty analogs of the TOW, capable of shoulder or tripod launch—81-millimeter mortars that could be set up to drop fire inside the compound, and a SADARM-ILS top-attack rig for use against roving en-emy armor. These had proven highly effective on One's mission into Yugoslavia to destroy SAM missile TELs sometime before.

The 1-Patchers of Boogie also had two guardian angels in the form of AH-1W Whiskey Cobras that had been assigned the troop for offensive and supporting fire during the attack. The AH-1Ws were shadowing the unit as it approached the target.

The presence of the helos was a time-saver, the added security they offered making it feasible for the mechanized troop to use the Rasif-Najawa highway that ran close to Al Athmidi instead of navigating open desert.

If a stink brewed up, the Whiskey Cobras could stamp it "canceled" in a hurry.

The mechanized force rolled on toward its objective, the ground elements keeping in contact with the two trailing gunships while themselves keeping a weather eye cocked for trouble that might materialize from the outlying desert or the road.

There were a lot of wadis in the vicinity, some of them deep, twisting, meandering ravines cut by flash-flood waters. It was possible in theory for unfriendly patrols to be holed up somewhere inside them and remain unseen by either the helos or the 1-Patchers until friendly troops were practically right on top of them.

Saxon steeled himself for a hard landing. The stick of HALO chutists that had walked from the hold of a C-130 two hundred miles away and a few thousand feet up was now nearing the end of its long, tapering, downward glide.

Limned in his head-mounted display, hardly twenty feet below and directly ahead of him, lay the south corner of the As Salima presidential palace that was the strike's primary target. The light-amplifying screen in front of him showed that the darkened landing zone was clear of troops and other combat hazards.

The complex was now under attack by 1-Patcher ground and heliborne elements. Gorilla's mechanized infantry forces were converging on the palace from the opposite end while the single AH-1W fired missile strikes and automatic cannon at targets of opportunity, drawing defensive fire in its direction while the paraforce dropped in unseen like Santa down the chimney.

Saxon's HMD displayed alphanumeric readouts in three colors. The blue altitude line similar to a fighter cockpit's dropped between numeric brackets to show the rate of descent. The relative positions of the other members of the paratroop detail were displayed as small human symbols in red, relative to the wearer's position in yellow.

Saxon keyed his lip-mike and gave the troop last-minute instructions before they hit the ground running. By now the chutist stick was only a few feet above the rooftop level of the multistory apartment block rising up from the south end of the mini-city.

As Saxon dropped below the level of the roof parapets, he could see inside some of the windows of the upper floors where lights dimly shone. But his attention was now tightly focused on the bare ground in front of him and his thoughts raced ahead to what had to be done very quickly during the next few minutes.

While making their descent, the paratroops were as vulnerable as clay pigeons at a skeet-shoot, but they would be more vulnerable still as they hit the ground and shucked their chute harnesses, disoriented and slowed by the changeover to land combat. Saxon, like all the others, had to stay agile and alert.

Within seconds, Saxon was down on the ground, strik-

ing the paved surface with both feet and simultaneously
pulling the quick-disengagement handgrip to get rid of the
chute which was now a major encumbrance. With a quick
tug on the handgrip, the parafoil broke away and scudded
along the pavement in the direction of the wind.

Saxon immediately had his main weapon, an AKS-74
with an under-mounted M-203 grenade launcher, in his
tactical-gloved hands, moving quickly to a defensive position to get clear of the other 1-Patchers coming down
behind him and to cover their flanks while they too un-
harnessed on the ground.

As he watched the airborne element come gliding down
all around him, a muted warble sounded in his ear and
one of the soldier icons on his NVG display flashed blue,
signaling a transmission from a member of the para force.

"Blue Man in position."

"You're not supposed to be. How'd you get there?"
Saxon returned.

"Boss, I figured the rooftop was just big enough to take
the chance, and it was so close I couldn't resist. So here
I am."

Blue Man was the team's sniper designation. Blue Man
had orders to enter the multistory apartment block at the
center of the complex once it was deemed secure and then
go to the rooftop to cover and spot for the team.

Blue Man was equipped with a Heckler & Koch
Präzisionsschützengewehr-1 (PSG1) sniper rifle with a
very accurate digital scope developed by DARPA to re-
place the standard Hensoldt 6 × 42 LED-enhanced scope
and manual reticle. Blue Man would be able to pick off
or pin down *Sai'qa* that 1-Patcher ground elements might
not be able to spot.

But Blue Man wasn't supposed to be up there yet, not
without a team having first secured the building. Still,

there he was. Saxon told him to stay alert and report in at regular intervals. He'd be informed when a security detail would be in the building to provide security backup.

Meanwhile the rest of the chutist stick was almost fully landed. So far there was no hostile engagement with the paratroops. The diversionary assault fire from Gorilla and the helo—codenamed Angry Falcon—was obviously doing its intended job, and it was clear to Saxon that said fire was intensifying as the defenders responded with a fierce resistance.

The *Sai'qa* were not Special Republican Guards. They were regular Iraqi army. But they had received specialist forces training and been awarded the right to wear the maroon berets of commando troops.

The *Sai'qa* had high morale and had been expected to put up tough and determined resistance once the attack commenced. But the Marine assault forces were far stronger and had struck with both speed and tactical surprise in their favor. They would prevail; of this Saxon had no doubt.

Saxon could now hear the sounds of the Marines' 81-millimeter mortar shells landing at the other end of the palace grounds. Every time one hit, the earth trembled slightly and the salvos of Iraqi small arms fire suddenly halted.

Saxon smiled grimly. He wasn't surprised. Few weapons of war could put the damper on a mud-soldier's fighting spirit than dropping some mortar cans on top of his head. All it took was the sight of what one mortar shell could do to the human body to make the survivors drop everything and take cover when the ripping silk sound preceded the next salvo.

He almost pitied Saddam's maroon beanies. He could picture them scuttling for cover as the fire came hurtling down on them. But such was war, and fuck them anyway; better they were on the receiving end than his own men.

By now all of the paratroop force was fully deployed on the ground. They had jettisoned their chutes and harnesses and were ready for action. Saxon's people knew the drill backward and forward by now, and were already methodically going about their appointed tasks.

Some were unshipping Claymore mines they'd carried in with them, crimping caps, unwinding det wires, and setting up the convex antipersonnel mines for remote detonation. Others were forming up into mobile assault squads and getting ready to do some fast-and-dirty door kicking. One of those details was on its way to secure the multistory apartment building with Blue Man already set up on the roof.

Saxon keyed his comms and called up the assault team.

"Stingray, this is Magic Dog. We are down and dirty. Say your situation."

"We are shit hot and ready to kick some fucking ass, boss. And I thank the Lord above for making me a Marine. God bless the U.S. Marine Corps."

It was Sgt. Mainline at the other end of the link. Saxon rogered that transmission as he heard the steady pounding of automatic weapons fire punctuated by the sporadic explosions of heavier armament in the background. Mainline went on to quickly and succinctly give an account of the shape of the battle so far.

"We've just breached the enemy's forward security defenses. Marines are already penetrating the palace grounds and setting up a security perimeter. Friendly casualties have been extremely light."

"Let me know if things change. Otherwise, go the whole nine yards."

"Fuckin' A, boss."

Hardly had Saxon broken contact with Stingray than
Blue Man came back on the net with an update.

"Activity on the rooftop of the building to your left."

Through his infra-red magnifying nightscope Blue Man
watched Iraqis setting up a machine gun emplacement on
the flat of the roof. "It's OK to look, Boss. You won't
see anything, though."

Saxon cautiously craned his neck. He didn't.

"Take them down," he ordered.

"Consider them wasted, Boss."

Blue Man was already drawing a bead on the head of
the bereted NCO who was ordering the other troops
around as they set up the MG. Others were piling sand-
bags in front of it and hauling in ammo crates.

The shot was near the limit of the PSG1's six-hundred-
meter range, but still well enough inside it for Blue Man
to be confident of making it. Windage was favorable too.
With his target in the crosshairs, Blue Man squeezed off
a round. The gun bucked once as the 7.62×51 millimeter
bullet exited the weapon's polygon-bored heavy barrel at
a muzzle velocity many times higher than conventional
rifles produced, while its low-noise bolt closing feature
reduced the sound of the shot to a low-decibel, subsonic
crack.

Almost instantaneously a red blossom appeared where
the bridge of the nose had once been on the face of the
Iraqi NCO on the distant roof as the heavy slug impacted,
crushing bone and cartilage and plowing a track through
brain tissue clear to the base of the skull.

The Iraqis had only enough time to react to the sight
of their commander doing a spastic death jig. Some even
began to smile, thinking it was some kind of a joke by
the otherwise humorless noncom. But then they heard the
delayed crack of the subsonic round and knew what was

really happening as the Iraqi pitched sideways and sprawled over the edge of the rooftop, before Blue Man aimed and fired a second of the twenty hollow-nosed bullets in the PSG1's magazine.

Three quick trigger pulls later he had put as many additional rounds into three unfortunate members of the MG squad setting up on the rooftop. The survivors had ducked down in panic, shouting and randomly firing rifle bursts in blind fear reactions. Two of them made the mistake of running toward the open door of the rooftop cupola, snapping off automatic AK salvos as they beat boot leather.

Blue Man dropped them in their tracks before they reached the cupola's dubious safety, and their twitching bodies served as an object lesson to the rest of the team who had wisely chosen to remain where they were. They were not about to go anywhere soon, but the muzzle flashes of their weapons had drawn the attention of Angry Falcon, which fired two Hydra rockets onto the rooftop, blowing the machine-gun emplacement apart and instantly killing all of the survivors.

Far below, Saxon's crew now began to deploy throughout the complex. The cat was out of the bag. The Fat Lady was singing her ass off. But the good guys were now on the ground, in position and ready to whale.

chapter *seventeen*

Some distance away, far beneath the desert crust, op-position forces were shrugging off surprise and the lethargy of sleep and preparing to counter the shock assault from air and ground.

Some units of the Iraqi Special Republican Guard are housed in underground bunkers scattered strategically across the Iraqi desert. The submerged complexes are buried about fifty feet below the surface crust. They are completely covered by two-foot-thick slabs of stressed concrete which extend approximately twenty feet beyond the edge of the complex, affording protection from missile strikes at any angle.

The bunkers, which apart from being hardened are segmented into modular units sheltering one hundred troops each, and with separate units for mess, sick bay, water, ammunition storage and the like, were designed for nuclear-chemical-biological warfare and built to specifications enabling them to sustain blast overpressure from up to a ten-megaton nuclear strike. Since the Gulf War, the bunkers—most of which survived Desert Storm intact—have been upgraded and extended, so that heavy vehicles and mechanized armor can be safely stored on-base.

It was in such a bunker complex beneath the desert that Special Republican Guard (SRG) troops were now rousing themselves to wakefulness and running to their war machines to mount up. The heavy concrete-and-steel blast door that protected a steeply sloping ramp was raised on pneumatic pistons.

From deep within the darkness, like the growling of the spirits of the dead, came the throbbing of engines and the clanking of armored caterpillar treads as the VII Mechanized Brigade rolled up onto the floor of the desert. The brigade belonged to the feared Al-Tikriti Division and it flew the banner of its national leader's home village. With sleep now a memory, the brigade was eager for battle. Tonight they would bring glory to their standard.

On its way to the Al Athmidi complex, Boogie was well clear of the Iraqi VII Brigade's line of advance, since the main force of the SRG was preoccupied with reaching the As Salima presidential palace, which, according to reports, was under attack by a sizeable paratroop force. Nevertheless, Boogie was to come under fire by a far smaller platoon-sized element of *Sai'qa* that was lurking just beyond the downslope of a deep wadi athwart the Marines' line of advance.

In the wake of sporadic yet insistent special operations strikes against Iraqi WMD facilities located in the vastness of the desert reaches, the general staff in Baghdad had opted to deploy small mobile units in strategic locations.

These light commando forces were downsized but heavily armed and, for Iraqi troops, well trained.

Each motorized desert platoon was equipped to fight spoiling attacks and stage ambushes against Western counter-WMD units sent into Iraq. They had studied the enemy's methods of operation and had trained hard.

They were motivated, their unit morale was high and many of their troops were seasoned desert fighters. So it was not much of a surprise that neither Hirsh's Boogie Force, or the two Whiskey Cobra gunships spotted the telltale silhouette of the camouflaged periscope that poked its way up from above the crest of a sandy rise. Behind it, a spotter peered at the oncoming formation through one of the newest and most accurate night vision scopes that Iraq had imported from Germany.

Minutes later, Boogie was suddenly taking fire from seemingly everywhere at once. The jackhammering of automatic weapons began to fill the air and an RPG rocket strike came shrieking in, blowing up a HUMVEE, killing the Marines inside and cooking off the stored armaments it carried, including the TOW missile in its roof-mounted launcher.

As the Hummer burned, the rest of Boogie ate gravel and took up defensive positions. The chattering of small arms fire intensified as 80-millimeter mortar shells now rained down on the Marines with the characteristic sound of zippers opening, to explode near the armored vehicles.

The mortars initially fell wide of the mark, but the Iraqis in the mortar pit were getting updates from a spotter behind binoculars flat against the top of a desert rise, and they were beginning to walk their fire toward the center of the massed enemy armor.

The Iraqis were clearly intent on slugging it out, because from out of the wadi came two BMP-2s, front-mounted 30-millimeter cannons blazing away while machine-gunners poured 7.62-millimeter automatic fire at the Marine invaders. By this time, though, Boogie's Bradleys were answering with their own 25-millimeter cannons, coaxial MGs and TOW ATGMs. In the course of the battle one of the Bimps took a TOW hit broadside, catching fire and going up in a whooshing fireball that rained down charred body parts and burning debris.

By now the two backup Angry Falcon AH-1Ws had overflown the combat zone and were cooking off missiles into the unfriendlies' positions.

The mortar pit was taken out by a salvo of Redeye missile strikes from one chopper, while the surviving Bimps were set ablaze by the other helo. As every veteran infantry crunchy knows, one drawback of mortars is that being short-range artillery weapons, they make easy targets for counter-mortar air. The *Sai'qa* in the now blazing mortar pit had been taught this lesson the hard and permanent way.

The battle was extremely brief, but it was also very bloody. It had whittled down Boogie's forces and had caused many friendly casualties. Now the Marine unit's target installation would surely also be on the alert. Still, Boogie had no option except to push on, taking friendly dead—or what was left of some—with it in human remains pouches. The enemy the troops just left to the whims of the buzzards and the hot desert sun.

Saxon's forces were meanwhile mopping up resistance from other Iraqi special ops detachments at the presidential palace, many of whom were putting up fanatical

resistance. Either they had been threatened with death if
they failed to halt the advance, or their objective was to
stall the consolidation of the base by unfriendly forces
until Iraqi reserves from VII Mechanized SRG arrived.

Probably the defenders' motivation was a mixture of
both, Saxon decided. The JSTARS surveillance aircraft
orbiting just across the Iraqi border in Saudi was reporting
the approach of a battalion-sized mobile force over MF-
1's TRAVLER global-mobile C4IFTW (C4I for the Warrior) system, so their morale might have been bouyed by
reports that help was on the way.

The GSMs or ground station modules (a mobile com-
panion rig on the ground containing radar and communications equipment needed to calibrate the movements
and positions of the ground forces JSTARS tracked), had
been moved close to the border. The GSMs were near
enough to Iraq to bring the ops zone in range of Joint
STARS' scopes.

JSTARS, unlike AWACS, didn't operate with an air
component alone, because it was one thing to track objects
in the skies as AWACS did, but another to be flying hundreds of miles slant-range of ground-based targets and
thereby fall victim to false returns common to slant-
ranging. The airborne component of JSTARS was only
one-half of the system; it was actually a ground/air
system.

Saxon was not surprised either by the heavy defensive
resistance or the new intel that enemy troops were ad-
vancing. Contingency plans had included the very obvious
and distinct possibility that a battalion of invading Americans might just happen to alert Iraqi forces to the fact
they were coming under coordinated attack. Sand Viper's
OPPLAN took this development—and other, even worse,

scenarios—into consideration and provided for extraction under fire, should such become necessary.

In the meantime, whatever jokers Saddam was about to deal MF-1 were still far enough away to worry about later. Right now, the force had its work cut out for it.

Saxon's assault troops were home free in some places, bogged down under fire in others, and mopping up suppressed resistance in yet others still. Blue Man was still on his rooftop, commanding a bird's-eye view of the unfolding developments on the ground, while the building itself was in the hands of a 1-Patcher security detail, part of whose role was to set up an O.P. and aid Blue Man as spotters from above.

On Saxon's end of the fight, the perimeter was already in friendly hands. Saxon wasted no time in joining one of the squads that were hunting for the supergun tubes and/ or hybrid ammunition thought to be hidden somewhere on the estate. Saxon had been back-briefed and knew where the likely hiding places might be located.

His crew's job was to clear those hiding places of opposition, carefully search them and destroy any weapons of mass destruction that were discovered.

Three squads had been assigned the task of locating and destroying weapons of mass destruction and precision machinery found on the estate. These squads, numbering six Marines each, now hit their assigned search areas.

Each squad had been briefed in what the search areas were suspected of harboring, in the type of threats they might face and in what to do if they found anything. From downloaded satellite imagery, sand table models had been constructed. The squads had used the models to help plan their ends of the mission, and had also used the Marines' computerized MARSFORCE mission planning system.

In all cases special equipment, such as ROC-1 NBC agent detectors, were carried by squad members. The handheld units could analyze even microscopic samples of NBC agents including chemical and biological toxins and radioactive isotopes used in nuclear warheads.

The squads were also equipped with full MOPP-6 level protective gear, which was not as cumbersome as the old-style gear. Most of the protective gear was kept stowed in their rucks so it wouldn't compromise troop mobility. If toxic or radioactive agents needed special handling, weapons disposal teams would suit up and go to work while their buddies secured the area.

Saxon hitched up with A-Squad, whose objective was the domed central structure at the southern sector of the palace. This was thought to be less a building than an elaborate shell to house and conceal a working prototype of the largest of the big artillery tubes Saddam was suspected of harboring here.

Though its objective appeared undefended, A-squad inched up carefully. Doing it by the numbers, one team was positioned to provide cover fire while a door-kicker squadron took the point for the actual assault.

Even up close, the Marines met no resistance. The building appeared unoccupied, its doors unlocked and swinging freely open. Just to make sure, a two-man team pitched frag grenades into the interior, ducking back behind the colonnades fronting the entrance as the grenades exploded with multiple *ka-rumps* somewhere inside. When the smoke and debris cleared, Chicken Wire came rushing in hurling blindfire from his M60E3 MG this way and that. Yet there remained no sign of defensive personnel and the area was pronounced secure.

STRIKE VECTOR 215

Saxon ordered A-squad to deploy into the building, but
warned his troops to look sharp and watch out for booby
traps. One too-green Marine, about to kick in a door, paid
no attention to the major's shouted warning to hold off,
and then it was too late. As the sole of his boot made
contact, the door blew off its hinges, taking with it most
of the foot that had kicked it. A few ounces of plastic
explosive had been hidden just behind the door, the detonator triggered by a mercury tilt-switch sensitive to the
slightest vibration. As a medic rushed over, the legless
paraplegic lay moaning and bleeding on the terrazzo.

On the building's belowground level, other squad elements were suddenly taking fire. Apparently there were
Iraqi troops inside the multilevel building, most of which
was underground, after all.

The fire came from enemy who had taken shelter in the
base as the attack unfolded, hoping to evade discovery.
Now that they'd been discovered, they'd decided to shoot
it out rather than surrender, but they were apparently not
well-trained as commandos and porting small arms only.

Some of these troops did surrender after more fire was
traded, but others had no intention of being taken alive.
One Iraqi ran straight into a group of Marines, detonating
two grenades in a suicide attack, shouting, "Vengeance!
Vengeance!" in Arabic. He took three of Saxon's crew
with him to wherever it was he thought he was going—
heaven, hell or neither.

Minutes later, Saxon was blowing a door off its hinges
with a bullpup shotgun blast, using a special door-busting
power load. Behind the door there lay a vast storeroom.
The big artillery tube was there—almost. Sections of
metal, ranging from the components of a large supercan-
non, to the same crated heavy artillery tubes that had been
videotaped by MF-1 in the Elburz mountains the previous

month were stacked here and there on the concrete floor.

But there was nothing else. And there was no functional weapon in place. The team had come up empty. This was a dry hole.

B-Squad found its objective and secured it without a shot being traded. Moonlight streamed in through the shattered windows as the team fanned out through the interior of the low-rise cinderblock building, their weapons at the ready, alert for the tripwires of booby traps, the silhouettes of snipers on the catwalk above or other signs of danger.

But the place had the look and smell of dereliction and disuse about it and they met no challenge. The bare cement floor was strewn with debris ranging from discarded food wrappers to yellowed newspapers that had been left to rot and mildew. The four corners also had obviously been used as toilets, and it was obvious from the stench that this use was of recent vintage. Apart from this, there was no sign of human habitation.

The Marines of B-Squad continued to search through the interior of the single-story building, looking for concealed rooms or entrances to hidden belowground workshops or storage bunkers. In the end, their efforts yielded nothing and the area was judged secure.

What the squad did turn up was indications that stockpiles of mass-destruction weapons components had been stored here until fairly recently. Abrasion marks on the concrete floor showed that forklifts and heavy loaders had probably been working in the warehouse structure only a short while ago.

Moreover, the ROC-1 sniffers showed minuscule traces of NBC contaminants in the air, with concentrations absorbed in the porous concrete where stacks of crates were thought to have been piled.

But now—nothing.

Another dry hole.

It was no cakewalk for C-Squad, which found itself facing determined resistance from within its search objective. The fire started up well before the Marines had approached the multistory white-brick building, forcing the detail to scramble for cover. A couple of Marines had been hit by the fusillade and the 1-Patcher medic attached to the unit had his hands full treating the wounded, especially because the pill-roller himself was taking fire as he ran to attend them.

C-Squad was pinned down behind the low, decorative stone walls and manicured plane trees that lined the gently curving walkways that led up to the building. It was obvious that an Iraqi defensive unit had dug in here and was expecting an attack, because the fire was accurate and well coordinated.

Fire lanes had obviously been mapped out in advance by an officer who knew his business, and sniper teams on the roof and in the windows of the multistory building were shooting as if they knew exactly where to place their rounds. There was undoubtedly a spotter or spotters somewhere high up who could call in fire by means of grid coordinates.

As the minutes ticked by, Marines on the ground were getting picked off by the Iraqis holding the building. C-Squad was left with one option, and that was to call in Angry Falcon. 1st Sgt. Spudder, the squad's commander, didn't like to have his dirty work done for him by helo-jockeys, but it was either get some air in fast or fall back under intense fire, taking more casualties in the process.

The Whiskey Cobra on loan to the assault force vectored in for the strike a few minutes later. Almost instantly it came under attack from the Iraqi pom-pom gun emplacement on the roof. They had set up a Norinco 20-millimeter triple-A rig with enough range to hit the chopper if it came in too close. The triple-A crew was pumping out red tracer fire at the helo with a will to vengeance.

It was notoriously hard to ignite an aircraft's fuel tanks with ordinary rounds, but with a salvo of phosphorus-coated 20-mike-mike, you could certainly do it. The AH-1W's pilot made sure to keep his bird well out of range of the slug-spitting Chinese coaxial gun on the roof for that one good reason.

And so, from a hover at standoff range, the pilot uncaged one of the helo's Redeye missiles, got a firing solution and launched the bird. Seconds later, the missile slammed into the roof, its 40-pound shaped-charge warhead exploding with tremendous impact in the center of the gun emplacement. The troops were blown literally to bits, heads and limbs ripped from their torsos and hurled to and fro by the force of the powerful explosive concussion.

The chopper then turned its malevolent attentions on the troops stationed on the upper levels of the building below the now vigorously burning roof. The Iraqis were at this stage pouring everything from Kalashnikov fire to 40-millimeter canister grenades at the chopper, hoping to knock the airborne predator out of the sky before it killed them all. Automatic fire strobed the windows with flame.

Darting this way and that like a gigantic black mosquito, the AH-1W raked the side of the building with its under-nose mounted 20-millimeter chain gun, thousands of glowing tracers spurting in a deadly arc across the entire facing wall, shattering glass and chewing up the interior of the rooms. All enemy fire from those uppermost floors was rapidly suppressed. As the Iraqis either ran or were taken out, and their shooting tapered off, the Whiskey Cobra just hung there, swaying slightly as it poured out fire. The heavy caliber rounds from the slaved, electrically driven, tri-barreled machine gun just kept chewing up walls and furniture, reducing everything in sight to splinters amid a cloud of dust and exploding debris.

Below, on the ground, C-squad's Marines now had their blood up and were eager to join the fray. Cheering like madmen and howling like banshees, they rushed the building, taking incoming automatic rifle and light machine gun fire as they charged hellbent for leather. Several 1-Patchers dropped in their tracks and never got up again. Their buddies ran forward, automatic rifles blazing at the hip in vengeful anger. As they breached the building's lobby, the fighting deteriorated into close-order combat in a narrowly confined space.

Those on both sides who had bayonets fixed to their rifle muzzles now used these ancient offensive weapons without hesitation or mercy. Opposing troops engaged each other in a combination of point-blank gunfire and fierce bayonet stabs into the throats, chests and abdomens of their antagonists.

The fighting was hard, fast and viciously savage, with heavy casualties developing on both sides. After the dust cleared, the Marines found they had prevailed. They then went about the business of taking prisoners and counting friendly and unfriendly dead. Fresh reinforcements were called in, and these soon began circulating through the building, taking still more casualties from booby traps, snipers and enemy diehards as they conducted door-to-door and floor-by-floor security actions.

It was in the basement of this building that an element of the now beefed-up force (it had started out as only C-Squad, but as the fighting intensified, more men had been poured in until its ranks had swelled to near-company strength by the time the building fell) encountered something, and made a discovery that was to change the complexion of the entire mission.

It was not what they had expected to find or anything with which they had been trained to deal. They did not encounter any of the weapons of mass destruction that they had been drilled to detect and destroy. Instead, the 1-Patchers came under suicidal fire from an entirely unexpected direction.

The building had a large underground parking area that ran its entire length. Except for the odd vehicle parked here and there, the garage was deserted. But under the dim glow of overhead mercury vapor lamps—many had been shot out to deliberately darken the area—the Marines saw a large 18-wheeler of a kind used internationally to transport containerized cargo.

Hardly had this discovery been made than they were suddenly taking fire from the truck.

The beefed-up C-squad, now C-detachment, went into action, immediately deploying to counter the determined fire from the truck. With superior numbers in the Marines' favor, the engagement was one-sided and brief. The firefight reached its climax when one of the shooters emerged from inside the cab of the big rig, from where he had been pouring fire at C-detachment, and advanced toward the Americans, pumping out grenades from an undermounted rifle launcher to cover his clip changes.

While he threw cans at the Marines, he shouted something in Arabic that might have been intelligible to one of the native speakers that manned each assault element, had it not been drowned out in the din of battle. Minutes passed and more fire was traded, until a multiround burst caught the gunman in his chest and he went down in a bloody heap. Then the Marines loped in to secure the truck.

Inside they found nothing to explain the suicidal resistance they'd encountered. The truck was empty except for some large packing crates and corrugated cardboard cartons, some of which had ostensibly contained bulky home appliances. There was nothing in the truck worth dying for, as far as any member of the team could surmise.

There was something else though—the Iraqi soldier who had attacked them, shouting oaths and seeking martyrdom, was still alive when the Marines reached him.

He didn't stay that way for long. He somehow managed to bite something taped to his wrist and died in a shuddering paroxysm of flailing arms and lashing legs. To make it all even stranger, it was now discovered that he had been firing a Galil, an Israeli-manufactured automatic rifle which closely resembled the AK-varients used by the Iraqis. His uniform also presented the 1-Patchers with an enigma, as it was not an Iraqi uniform. The soldier was garbed in Israeli battle dress, his fatigues bearing a patch with a six-pointed star.

The squad leader immediately called up Saxon on the force's SINCGARS radio net. The boss would want to know about this ASAP.

chapter *eighteen*

The ruined, sandblasted and time-stained concrete buildings were scattered throughout the dusty corner of the desert, a mere stone's throw from the highway. The area was known to the long-haulers who traveled the route as a truck park, the modern-day equivalent of the caravansaries that had dotted the ancient Middle East.

The structures, first erected during the 1960s as pumping stations along a now derelict oil pipeline stretching between Baghdad and Amman, had long ago been abandoned, and the heavy equipment that had filled them scrapped. For decades the remaining concrete shells had been used by long-haul truckers as refuges from the *shamal*, bandits and the biting desert cold, places to sleep off the fatigue of the road in relative safety or to perform makeshift repairs to their rigs.

This morning the old pumping station was empty, the concrete shells of defunct pump houses sitting abandoned and forlorn beneath the pale light of the setting moon. Yet in the distance there now arose a sound familiar to the wayfarers who frequented this place. The rumbling of powerful diesel truck engines began to be faintly heard. A truck convoy was drawing near.

Above the keening of the wind, the rumbling steadily rose in pitch and intensity. Before long, the sound of the approaching diesel-powered leviathans rolling from the highway onto the flattened earth between the buildings had reached a deafening crescendo. Soon the rectangular black shapes, showing only amber and red running lights, stopped, their airbrakes squealing, their motors sputtering and coughing as the drivers killed the ignitions.

Doors were thrown open and men with muscles cramped from long, tedious hours of sitting in crowded cabs emerged into the night, stretching and rubbing their hands against the chill air. As they emerged, some of these men eyed their former traveling companions surreptitiously, stealing up close behind them as they reached into the pockets of their coats for the peg-ended steel wire garrotes they carried concealed there.

Soon the muffled screams and choking death rattles of the unfortunates were whipped away by the rising desert wind, and the bodies hidden in the utter darkness that followed moonset. With sunrise, the buzzards would scent the carrion, and begin to circle.

Caught in the middle of a nasty firefight before its objective, Boogie was pinned down on the desert by Iraqi defense cadre. Earlier on, in the surprise attack by *Sai'qa* forces, the unit had received its baptism under fire, and its men were in no mood for gratuitous heroics. All they wanted now were results, and the only casualties they were willing to accept were the enemy's.

And so nobody complained about Angry Falcon air support stealing the glory when the choppers were called in to soften up the enemy's defenses. This they did speedily, rocketing and shooting up the installation with their nose cannons and missiles. Within a short span of time the target objective was reduced to a mass of blazing ruins.

Boogie then moved in to secure the area. The Marines encountered small arms fire, savage in some parts of the base, but not on an order of magnitude that the invading force was not well-equipped to handle.

Now Boogie hived off into separate squads of mechanized and straight-leg ground patrols. The armor rushed in ahead of the foot troops, plowing 25-millimeter cannon fire, heavy MG salvos and LAW and TOW ATGW rocket strikes into enemy gun emplacements and Iraqi armor. The AH-1W helos continued to circle, shooting up the steel pylon supporting the base radio mast and sending the antenna dishes clustering its upper tier crashing to the ground. The choppers also shot up the upper floors and rooftop of a large building that was being used as a sniper nest by Iraqi defenders.

Because of the stiff opposition, the teams were not able to secure the compound for the better part of an hour. Then they fanned out to complete their recon by fire. Yet here too, they discovered nothing.

Here too the installation had turned out to be a dry hole.

The non-military vehicles, mostly high-end SUVs, flew the flags of the Iraqi Ba'ath Party and the Revolutionary Command Council, the latter defined by the Iraqi Constitution as the supreme legislative and executive authority of the state. Anyone daring to attempt to stop the motorcade would have been shown a pass signed by the highest ranking members of Baghdad's ruling elite. The rights of a holder of such a pass could not be dismissed, and the name of the questioner would have been taken down for later investigation by the GID and the inevitable punishment which would follow such an investigation.

But there had been no opposition on the road, and the vehicles that made up the motorcade ate up the miles. Driving hard, they reached their destination shortly before sunup.

Dr. Jubaird Dalkimoni saw to his relief that the truck convoy had arrived before him exactly as planned. The bodies of those who would not have the honor of martyring themselves for the holy cause were scattered on the ground. This too had been expected. The others, the Trusted Ones, had done their work swiftly and well—as they had been trained to do.

Dalkimoni emerged from the rear of the air-conditioned limousine and stepped toward the men who were waiting in a small semicircle, prepared to greet him. They had built a fire in an old oil drum, burning trash to make a wan flickering flame adequate to warm their hands against the receding night's chill.

Dalkimoni smiled as he approached them, opening his arms to enfold the first of the men at one end of the crescent, and embrace him as a brother in arms. Soon, he thought, as he moved to the second man in line, they would all be going to a place where such contrivances would no longer be necessary.

With luck, many others would forever join them there.

Saxon had flagged down one of the assault force's HUMVEEs and ridden the almost half-mile distance to the building that had been assaulted by C-Detachment. With a screech of tires, the Hummer rolled down the steeply graded ramp, soon disgorging the strike force's commander in the midst of the underground car park.

The place, which had been in semidarkness at the time of the firefight, was now well lit with sodium-arc lamps— part of the gear the Marines had brought along—powered by taps applied to the building's electricity. The truck and the bloodied corpses of the Iraqis who had defended it, stood out in stark detail, grimly lit by the harsh blue-white glare of the portable lamps.

Saxon was quickly briefed by the unit's leader and then had a look around for himself. As he surveyed the corpses strewn around the captured truck, Saxon had no doubt that the men who his Marines had surprised here had been about to embark on a covert behind-the-lines mission of some kind.

The Israeli uniforms and weapons that they ported alone bespoke this fact. The truck was found to have had mechanical difficulties, which explained its presence in the garage.

Inside the truck's cargo area, they found mounts on floor and ceiling for cargo that would require strong cushioning against the shock of rough desert road transport. There was no manifest of any kind, though, found inside the truck's cab or on the persons of the corpses, to describe what this cargo might have been.

All that Saxon knew for sure was that men had been prepared to die here, rather than surrender, and this fact told him that the cause for which they'd martyred themselves had to have been of great importance to them. The truck told him more as well. His mind flashed back to the road in Iran, flashed back to the team's undercover work in Germany earlier in the mission, flashed back to the high meadows of the Swiss Glarner Alps. There was surely a connection between this truck and the Bonn-Karachi truck convoy route. But what exactly? That question didn't yet have an answer.

The findings of the team equipped with NBC agent sniffers confirmed Saxon's growing fears, however. The sniffers showed heavy traces of chemical toxins and radioactivity clinging to the interior of the cargo bay. The truck had contained something extremely deadly and, to judge by the fittings in the cargo bay, fairly large and bulky. Saxon thought that there weren't too many things that fit that description—besides a bomb.

S axon had a difficult choice to make.

He now suspected that there had been other trucks, containing a dirty hybrid nuclear device, that had left the presidential palace for the same destination or destinations. But the unit's safety window was beginning to close. It was time to withdraw from the presidential palace. Satellite imaging showed a large contingent of Special Republican Guards on its way to stage an assault to take back the palace.

Marine Force One could not permit itself to be trapped here. The invasion's personnel requirements had been calculated to be sufficient to storm and secure the As Salima presidential palace. The force could not prevail in a siege situation with as many troops as the Iraqi military chose to throw against it.

The V-22 Ospreys that were to evacuate Marine Force One were already in flight from Oman. The convertiplanes, which had refueled over the Persian Gulf, had a current ETA of fifteen-plus minutes. Saxon's teams were already forming up in the compound, ready to embark on landing. Saxon had his orders: they were to evacuate along with the rest of his Marines.

But as the final V-22 came in to pick up the troops, Saxon issued entirely different orders. A platoon-sized detachment of hand-picked volunteers was to fly toward the highway in the Osprey with Angry Falcon AH-1W support. It was to search for any large trucks it found similar to the one in the underground car park and destroy them after warning the drivers to evacuate. If capture seemed imminent, the Marines were to blow the aircraft and themselves up rather than surrender to the Iraqis. Saxon and his volunteers had now also found a cause worthy of martyrdom.

J ubaird Dalkimoni walked to the first of the four trucks, to inspect the precious cargo it carried onboard. He actually needed only two of these big lorries; the others were for backup in the event that the first two failed for some reason to perform as expected. Yet a fifth truck had malfunctioned, and its cargo offloaded to one of the present vehicles, he had learned; but this possibility had been anticipated, thus the redundancy built into the plan.

The operation, Dalkimoni knew, would be his crowning achievement, and would represent a major victory for the *Rais*.

Saddam Hussein would in the end emerge victorious in an uneven conflict with the Western democracies that had lasted almost a decade-and-a-half.

The victory would bring incalculable glory to the Iraqi leader. It would destroy the American presence among the Arab states of the Gulf and it would pour the holy fire of Islam's righteous wrath down upon the Israelis in a bloodbath unequaled by anything in antiquity, just as the *Rais* had promised long ago.

In the first dull glimmers of early morning, Dalkimoni stepped into the first truck to inspect the cargo. The false fronts of the packing crates had been moved aside by his soldiery, and the smooth metallic surface of one of the Winged Bulls of Nebuchadnezzar was exposed to his view.

Beautiful, awesome, he thought. A beauty as terrible and fierce as that of the desert sun that was now rising over the land to cast its scalding rays across the parched and desolate earth.

Since prehistory, men here had worshipped that celestial power, and now Dalkimoni would unleash that same elemental force in the service of his country and his cause. He could now die, in the knowledge that the culmination of everything to which he had devoted his life was about to be realized in a single obliterating flash of terrible glory.

Dalkimoni moved closer within the confining shadows of the truck's cargo hold. He reached out to touch the ovoid weapon slung between the welded steel cocoon of its support assembly. Such protection against shock was necessary to ward off premature detonation. The nuclear explosives were sensitive to the slightest vibration. They were as delicate as eggs.

Yet these were dragon's eggs. The fiery beasts that would emerge from them would consume the Middle East, changing it for a thousand years. They were indeed that consuming fire that Saddam had promised years before, during the cowardly attacks of the Western coalition's Desert Storm.

Then, the Leader had pledged that the Iraqi fire would eat up all of Israel. He had sworn this by Allah, sworn his holiest of oaths before the assembled nations of the earth, sworn it at the infidel warmonger in the White House with heroic defiance.

And the *Rais* had meant it. Had meant every word that he had uttered, there in the confines of his bunker beneath the presidential palace, that same bunker beneath the complex of buildings that had once been the U.S. Embassy in Baghdad.

Saddam was not like other men. Surely not like the cowardly Americans. He did not calculate his actions in days, weeks or months. He thought in terms of years, in decades, in centuries. Surely the Leader wove his plans for all eternity.

Saddam had known then that he was powerless against the United States' formidable technological might. But he had been ready to sacrifice for victory, and to plan even in defeat. Even then, the germ of his nuclear weapons program was taking root. Slowly, steadily, irresistibly, despite the brutal economic sanctions and the UN inspections imposed by the unfair peace treaty he had signed, the expertise and technology base grew.

In time, the four Winged Bulls—Al Assur, the Warrior; Al Tammuz, the Anointed; Al Gerra, the Fire Bringer and Al Samas, Lord of Light—had been fashioned from bomb-grade U-235 extracted by cascades of gas centrifuges hidden deep below the Leader's many presidential palaces.

And here they now were, these terrible weapons of glory. Ready for use against the hated enemies of the *Rais*.

Dalkimoni continued his inspection. The nuclear weapons were complete and perfect in every regard, except for the arming and blast initiation modules engineered from the Columbine Heads he had spirited with him to Baghdad. These he now screwed into special receptacles in each bomb casing. They were not yet armed, however, but they soon would be. For the time being, Dalkimoni issued instructions for his soldiers to move the false crates into position and to seal the trucks' cargo holds.

Then he approached the drivers. Those who would deliver the weapons were each given what Dalkimoni told them were "visas for heaven." On one side of each wallet-sized mylar card were printed the arming codes for the nuclear weapon onboard an individual truck. On the other side, prayers and greetings for the guardians of the gates of *Behesht Zahra*—heavenly paradise. On meeting these celestial gatekeepers they were to present their visas and gain admittance to an eternity of unceasing delight.

As to arming the weapons, they were instructed to do this just before crossing the two borders. The first would be detonated away to the east, inside Iran—this weapon's team carried the designation Al-Marduk. The second nuke would explode in the west, beyond the border crossing with Syria—Al-Tiamat was its team's designation.

Dalkimoni assured the drivers that the visa cards they carried would not fail to win them a place of honor in the next world. In heaven these cards would be read by the Prophet himself, and would instantly assure their bearers of the blessings reserved only for Islam's heroic *mujahideen*.

In their eyes, Dalkimoni saw that they truly believed every word he told them. That was good. The ration of hashish issued to each man would also help, the doctor well knew. It would make it easier for the simpletons to chew on the ration of bullshit about heaven he now expected them to swallow hook, line and sinker.

*　　*　　*

In the V-22 Saxon's team rotored low across the parched desert crust toward the rising sun. Meanwhile, the rest of the unit was extracting westward, to the safety of Drop Forge on the other side of the Jordanian border. Those on the way back had grumbled at deserting the boss, but Saxon had laid down the law, and they'd done as ordered.

Saxon's destination was the main trunk of the Baghdad-Amman highway. There, he might chance to interdict the route of the other trucks he suspected would form a convoy, as trucks usually did along the route.

He realized his strategy was a long-shot. Hell, it was worse than that. It was Quixotic and probably suicidal. On the other hand, what would you call who-knew-how-many nukes making their way across the highway? Genocidal. And genocide beat suicide any day of the week. Besides, what other option did he have? Calling in B-52 strikes against every truck in Iraq just wasn't going to cut it.

No. Saxon had to bet on those trucks being on the Amman-Baghdad stretch of the Bonn-Karachi truck route. It was the most likely place to find them in a region of the world where few highways existed capable of supporting heavy vehicle traffic. This fact alone brought the chance of locating the rigs within the realm of the possible. The highway amounted to the only transport corridor the trucks could use.

But then what? On this point Saxon figured he would just have to improvise.

The two Iraqi Mig-29 Fulcrums had been scrambled to deal with the escaping convertiplanes. Two of the Whiskey Cobra attack helos were along to ride shotgun, but they would be of little use against the speed, armament and sophisticated avionics of Russia's personal best.

This was especially so since, with covert Soviet retrofitting, the relatively few first-line MiG fighters that the Iraqi air force possessed had been upgraded with the latest that the Mikoyan Design Bureau had to offer. The planes were not only faster and more maneuverable than ever before, but they could be equipped with anybody's weapons, thanks to their hybrid missile launch rack systems. The wing strakes on the retrofitted Fulcrums could take French, British and American air-to-air or air-to-ground munitions, as well as natively manufactured Russian bombs and rockets.

Soon the MiG pilots closed with the escaping helos, which had split up and begun undertaking evasive maneuvers. The Fulcrums did too, each selecting its first target. The prioritizing was cut-and-dried here: The AH-1W Whiskey Cobras were the most dangerous, so they had to go first.

They were not about to go easily, though. Spotting the Fulcrums, one of the helos banked and got off two Redeye strikes before the MiG could return fire, causing the Fulcrum pilots to break left and right in order to evade the heat-seeking missile warheads.

When the Fulcrums came out of their defensive maneuvers, the escaping helos were no longer in visual range. The Fulcrums searched the skies, hunting their prey like the mechanical sharks they so closely resembled. They were not stymied for long. Their long-range threat identification radars soon got a target skin paint on a due west bearing.

Yes, they had them again.

This time the MiG pilots would not make the mistake of closing before firing. They would fire their French

Mistral-3 missiles at the weapons' maximum standoff range. The Whiskey Cobras were primarily tank- and armor-busters, never intended to undertake airborne combat. They possessed nothing like the radars of air dominance fighter planes such as MiG-29 Fulcrums. The MiG pilots simply kept out of range of the helos' weapons, put the pipper on their targets and pickled off their ordnance.

The Whiskey Cobras didn't stand a chance, and they soon were history. The missiles scored two good kills within a matter of seconds. Puffballs of orange-black fire marked the places in the sky where the Marine helos had flown, whole and intact, moments before. The choppers had completely disintegrated under the impact of the lethal air-to-air munitions strikes. There was just nothing left.

Now the Fulcrums went after the V-22 convertiplanes. Here they had even less to fear from their far slower and completely unarmed quarry. And here again, they could effectively engage and destroy the target from the limits of standoff range. The Fulcrum pilots selected AA-10 Alamo beyond-BVR-capable missiles, the next best in their hybrid warload, and uncaged the birds. The missiles began to track and in moments would be ready to launch.

The MiGs had only seconds left before destruction, however, though their pilots didn't yet realize it. A far deadlier and far stealthier opponent than even the Fulcrums had been tracking the fighter sortie through the skies and was about to launch an AMRAAM strike on each enemy plane.

Behind the sleek Plexiglas bubble canopies of the F-22 Raptors, the flight leader and his wingman had both acquired their targets, opened the internal weapons carriage doors and exposed the CSRL multiple launch racks so the AMRAAMs could uncage and complete the launch sequence. Now the Raptors' automatic fire control systems cooked off their birds.

The first and last intimation of the onset of death was the threat radars screeching out warning tones in the Fulcrum pilots' headsets. One moment they were about to fire on their slow-moving, unprotected targets, the next they themselves had come under surprise attack from a far deadlier foe. The MiG pilots broke sideward to evade, their own attacks automatically aborted because the uncaged missiles had not yet been ready to launch.

The two AMRAAM missiles closed with the bogies and detonated on impact, destroying the Fulcrums in a meteoric shower of metal and flame. High overhead, the Raptors streaked past the fireworks display on opposite bearings. One F-22 escorted the Ospreys toward the Jordanian border. The other fighter plane broke eastward, in search of the idiot jarhead major who the sortie had learned had gone off looking to win himself a posthumous Medal of Honor.

chapter *nineteen*

Saxon's problems were complicated by a *shamal* that had blown up during the convertiplane's low-altitude transit of the desert. The V-22 was of course equipped with advanced FLIR imaging modules, but forward looking infra-red is essentially a navigational and targeting aid, not a search tool. An effective airborne search effort requires a lot of visual scanning of the outlying terrain with the naked human eye, and field glasses where necessary.

The swirling clouds of sand and ice particles, blown by winds of often cyclonic velocity, also made keeping the V-22 airborne a test of the cockpit crew's skill, nerve, grit and determination. The Marines at the helm were scared shitless, but they kept right on flying into the teeth of the worsening weather system. None of them had ever encountered anything like this before, not in training or in combat. It was, in short, a gold-plated, died-in-the-wool, fifty-ton-gorilla-sized bitch.

The Osprey continued to fly on.

* * *

The prayers of supplication had been concluded. The Trusted Ones, those brethren beloved of Allah, rose from the dust of the desert floor, their outer clothing stained with ochre patches. In their eyes, Dalkimoni saw the telltale gleam of fanaticism.

He had never fully understood it. He had always loathed it. Sometimes, indeed quite often, he had feared it as the force of mindless destruction that it undoubtedly was.

But the doctor had always known that it could be used. Focused and directed like a laser beam, it was one of the primal, elemental forces of human nature, perhaps of the universe itself. It could and had toppled empires throughout the ages. Soon, very, very soon, it was to perform this miracle yet again.

The bomb-maker nodded at his bodyguard *Sai'qa*, provided by Qusay himself. They were to secure the area after the trucks departed. No sign of their presence—including the hapless ones who'd been killed—was to be left behind.

Then Dalkimoni and they would depart for Baghdad, there to await news of the developments that would take place within the space of a scant few hours. As the cool of the morning gradually changed to the fiery heat of the day, as the *shamal* dissipated and the desert sun rose to its zenith, other suns would rise. Suns of death—and vengeance long delayed.

The Marine piloting the Osprey angrily shook his head. The V-22 was running low on fuel. The convertiplane had limited avgas reserves and would have to turn around

real soon if the crew and passengers stood any chance of
reaching safety. Though the Osprey was equipped for air-
to-air refueling, though it could drink avgas from a KC-
10A through its nose-mounted refueling probe, it would
first have to cross over to the friendly side of the Saudi
or Jordanian border before filling up.

Fuelbirds preferred to dispense aviation gasoline at approximately twenty thousand feet. Flying the boom at this
altitude kept the fuel at the right pressure and temperature
to insure the maximum rate of dispersal, and also helped
prevent other things happening to the avgas, like the formation of ice crystals in the mix.

The maximum ceiling for tanker aircraft was about
forty thousand feet. This was a high ceiling for a tanker,
but a low ceiling for a SAM. A fuelbird coupled up with
a V-22 would be as easy a target for an Iraqi SAM as
two roaches fucking on the kitchen wall for a well-aimed
sneaker.

The bottom line was that the V-22 had to be over
friendly air before it had its drink. That was the long and
the short of it. The Osprey had been outfitted with additional onboard fuel storage capacity, but the aircraft
burned up hundreds of gallons by the minute, and flight
time had to be precisely calculated. Saxon understood the
equation. He knew that mere minutes remained to spot
those trucks, and if he didn't luck out, then the Fat Lady
had already sung, and that was it.

Then, with unexpected suddenness, through a break in
the swirling maelstrom of the *shamal*, he caught sight of
the dull glimmerings of white-painted rectangular objects
below. He thought there were numerical markings on
them, the kind trucks often had on their roofs; the kind
the captured lorry at the presidential palace had also displayed.

Saxon told the pilot to circle around for another look. As the convertiplane made a second pass, the swirling curtain of sand and ice parted enough to reveal the pumping station directly below.

To Saxon's relief the rectangular objects he'd spotted before turned out to be trucks.

Four of them.

Suddenly, and from out of nowhere, they had come under attack.

It was difficult to determine just who or what was shooting at them.

Dr. Jubaird Dalkimoni looked up, shielding his eyes, trying to piece together exactly what had happened. He'd heard the unmistakable sound of helicopter rotorblades. That much was clear. Through the parting sheets of whirling sand and driving sleet Dalkimoni could make out the bulky black shape weaving back and forth across the sky.

It was a helo.

Yes. A large one. Almost like a plane.

And he soon saw men fast-roping down from its open rear hatch.

Commandos!

The Israelis perhaps?

Or the Sons of Dogs, the Americans.

Still more likely.

Whoever it was, they would die. Thankfully, he had brought along a force of *Sai'qa* and they were ably trained. Let them now do their job.

"Shoot them! *There*! Above you!" Dalkimoni shouted, gesturing upwards.

Pulling a Skorpion machine pistol from the pit holster slung across his chest, Dalkimoni began firing three-round bursts at the invaders from the sky as if to lead by example. His wild, desperate shooting accomplished nothing, struck nothing. But it encouraged the others to go into action.

All at once defensive small arms fire started up from positions scattered throughout the truck stop. Glowing tracer bullets spat toward the hovering chopper from which human targets were emerging.

There were commandos descending on the truck stop. Americans. There was no mistaking it now. From glimpses of the enemy's chocolate-chip BDUs it was obvious they were under attack by U.S. troops.

The maroon berets worn by the assault force completed the picture. Special Forces. From where had they come? It didn't matter. They were here. Fight or be killed was the name of the game.

Dalkimoni's men took cover wherever they could, reloading and firing again and again as the final red tracers in sustained automatic bursts informed them that their ammo magazines were running dry. The 1-Patchers were now on the ground, outnumbered by unfriendlies. The unarmed Osprey cleared out, but the AH-1W's rockets and nose cannon evened the score considerably. Once One was down and engaged with the enemy, the fight moved away from the trucks, spilling over into the abandoned buildings of the pumping station.

In sum, it became a melee, with part of the Marine force up to its ears trying to take out the *Sai'qa* in fierce close-quarter combat, and the rest attempting to secure the nuclear weapons trucks before their hell-bent-on-suicide drivers were able to get them rolling onto the highway again.

* * *

Saxon glimpsed the familiar face of the Arab bomb-maker amidst the shifting, surging chaos of combat. It was just as pug-ugly as in the three-position Bertillon mugshot that the German cop Winternitz had shown him back at the safe house in Berlin. Now, Dalkimoni was hotfooting it to one of the motorcade's SUVs where the bloodied corpse of a bullet-pocked *Sai'qa* was slumped over the steering wheel.

The bomb-maker struggled to pull the heavy, dead weight from behind the wheel and dump the corpse onto the ground. While Dalkimoni was busy heaving the ca-daver, Saxon snapped off a burst of AK-74 fire and a brace of stub-nosed 5.45-millimeter bullets spanged and wheezed against the side of the cab, shattering glass and pockmarking metal. Unhanding the dead man, Dalkimoni quick-drew his Skorpion machine pistol and snapped off an answering nine-millimeter autoburst, forcing Saxon to drop down and kiss the sand.

When he rose back up again, Dalkimoni had ditched the troublesome corpse and was already behind the steer-ing wheel with the ignition roaring. The SUV was now barreling away from Saxon, peeling off smoking rubber as its tires screamed for purchase on the shifting sands. Saxon tried to shoot out the tires, but the marker tracers he'd loaded showed him the bullpup rifle's clip only had a few rounds left in it. So far none of them seemed to have inflicted any damage on the getaway car. Saxon tossed aside the now dry AK and unholstered his Beretta service sidearm, a double-action weapon he carried un-safetied and hammer-down in condition-one mode.

Gun drawn, Saxon bolted after the truck, nearly taking a hit from another volley of Skorpion autofire that Dal-kimoni backhanded his way out the driver's-side window. With the SUV still floundering in the sand, Saxon jumped onto the passenger-side running board and smashed the window to splinters with the receiver of this pistol, shards of safety glass peppering his face and temporarily blinding him.

As Saxon shook off the translucent blue flakes of shattered window glass, Dalkimoni leveled his machine pistol and fired a burst straight across the seat. Saxon ducked just in time to dodge the shot pattern as bullets went whipping past his head, triggering an answering Beretta round on the follow-through.

But nothing happened as the hammer dropped. The Beretta had apparently jammed and hung fire. Not surprising, the thought flashed through Saxon's mind—only an asshole would trust an automatic to function in the middle of a sandstorm after using it as a fire axe.

Saxon guessed that this clearly made him an asshole, but he could kick himself later. Right now he had a raging Arab terrorist pointing a Skorpion machinepistol at his head, and, unlike his own, the badguy's gun seemed to be working just fine.

Saxon ducked below the shattered window as a burst of hot lead punched through the space his head had occupied a moment earlier. He considered pitching a minigrenade into the cab and then jumping off the SUV, but at the reckless speed Dalkimoni was driving he'd probably wind up breaking his own neck. Besides, Saxon wanted Dalkimoni in one piece if he could at all arrange it. He had his own reasons for this.

Now the door went pock—pock—*pock*. Three steel rosebuds blossomed in quick succession to the right and left of the handle.

Then suddenly, from within the cab of the SUV, Saxon heard Dalkimoni howl in pain. Saxon intuitively knew what had happened. Dalkimoni had let his emotions overrule his common sense and continually aimed low to shoot right through the door frame hoping more easily to hit his opponent's vitals.

Inevitably one or more of the PB slugs he'd fired through the door had fragmented on impact. A ricocheting sliver of lead had probably hit him.

Saxon risked taking a Skorpion volley in the face and snapped back up to peer through the glassless window frame.

Sure enough, Saxon saw that Dalkimoni was bleeding from a wound above his left eye. Blood was pouring down his collar too. A slug fragment had gouged a chunk from his head, but it was a superficial wound. The bomb-maker was still very much alive and kicking. But at least he didn't have his gun anymore. In the heat of action he'd dropped it and it had tumbled out of reach.

With Dalkimoni now disarmed, Saxon tried to yank open the passenger door but it was locked from inside and the lock mechanism damaged by bullet strikes. Reaching in with his hand, Saxon tried to pull the frozen inner latch, dodging the wickedly sharp blade of a spring-loaded knife that Dalkimoni suddenly pulled from his pocket and with which he now tried to slice off Saxon's fingers as he one-handed the wheel.

But the swaying, lurching path of the SUV made it impossible to play Japanese sushi chef with Saxon's hand and control the vehicle at the same time. Saxon was finally able to get a sufficiently solid grip on the latch so he could apply enough leverage to yank open the door.

Saxon was soon in the passenger seat, the passenger door banging open and shut as its damaged lock prevented it from securing against the wildly careening vehicle. Dalkimoni's knife went clattering out the driver's window as both men grappled for it. The fight for control of the

SUV quickly degenerated into an ugly primal contest between two antagonists bereft of weapons, bereft of even
the ability to use combat skills in the tightly enclosed
space. It was now a clawing, punching, head-butting,
body-thrashing, arm-wrenching brawl. A death match
where grunts of struggle displaced words and stabs of
blinding pain replaced coherent thoughts.

In the end it was the SUV that decided the issue, and
the human combatants who had to abide by its judgment
call. Now Saxon's hands were on the wheel, now Dalkimoni's. And now again possession of the steering wheel
changed once more. In the end, the four-by-four careened
off the access road of the truck stop, fishtailed almost
completely around, and crashed head-on into the concrete
base of a steel electrical pylon located just off the highway.

The impact of the collision sent both men sprawling
against the dashboard, roof and doors, badly cut and ba-
tiked with blood as the truck's airbags inflated. The main
difference between them was that Dalkimoni had been
knocked unconscious in the collision while Saxon still had
his wits about him. Saxon figured that made him the win-
ner by default as he dragged the dazed bomb-maker out
of the wreckage by his feet.

By the time Saxon returned to the pumping station, the
Mean One had the area nailed down tight. Those
Sai'qa who had not been killed in battle were seated in a
line with their hands clasped behind their heads, watched
over by Marines with rifles pointed at their faces.

The wounded were either being treated by the team's
medic or were already aboard the V-22, while the Raptor,
which had found Saxon's detachment, flew a high-altitude

security CAP overhead. Bandaged and bloodied, in many cases, most of the Marine volunteers had survived the engagement and were grateful to be alive. Later, they would be called heroes, but Saxon would see that those who started bragging about it would no longer be part of One.

As for the rest—friendly and unfriendly KIAs were lined up on the desert crust in the burnished copper light of dawn. The only difference between them now was that the friendlies were being zipped into vinyl body bags while the unfriendlies were dragged inside the empty pumping station's blockhouses. Worms, snakes and scorpions would soon have their way with them there.

By the time Dalkimoni came around, he was securely handcuffed with cable ties and under guard with the rest of the Iraqi POWs. Saxon was over by the trucks, where his counter-WMD people with special technical training and equipment were completing an assessment of the nukes.

They had come to the As Salima presidential palace prepared to destroy weapons of mass destruction in place if necessary. The 1-Patchers had carried into combat with them special demolition charges developed by DARPA that were supposed to be able to accomplish this job with minimal risk of environmental contamination.

The charges were part plastic high-explosive, part incendiary. They were phased detonation charges, designed to surround a nuclear or biological/chemical weapon in a cocoon of blast, intense heat and overpressure sufficient to vaporize even plutonium weapon cores and the most virulent weaponized biologicals known to exist in the arsenals of rogue nations.

The one problem was that they had never been tested

in actual battlefield use, only in computer simulations. But there was a first time for everything.

As Saxon watched, the counter-WMD specialists were completing the placement of the charges on the nuclear weapons in all four of the captured trucks. The charges would be set for delayed time detonations to enable the helos to get clear of the blast, with a radio-controlled backup available in case the timers failed to work.

This was possible but not probable—the best timing electronics had gone into the timers, and they were multistage, so if one chip failed, two more ICs backed them up. Everything was redundant. It would fly.

With the nukes rigged to blow, Saxon gave the orders for the team to deploy. As for the captured Iraqi commandos, they were handed the keys to their vehicles and told what was about to happen. They had five minutes to put as much distance between themselves and the next Sodom and Gomorrah as they were capable of doing. The *Sai'qa* wasted no time in climbing into their SUVs and beating a path out of the pumping station, the wounded helped by those who had emerged from battle unscathed, the dead left behind without a second thought.

The sandstorm, which had abated, was again worsening somewhat. Yet now for the first time the V-22 pilot looked upon the *shamal* with equanimity, even something approaching welcome. The weather would help hide the multirole transport from Iraqi air and ground patrols, he surmised. And the powerful blasts from the det charges would also keep the enemy guessing.

Within minutes, loaded down with MF-1 personnel, the Osprey lifted off and translated to horizontal flight. The special-purpose charges detonated before the convertiplane had gotten more than a mile from ground zero.

On the horizon there arose a mushrooming pillar of fire

and luminous, billowing cloud that reached up to momentarily eclipse the sun, or so at least it seemed. Satellite sensors in space would later determine that the fissile pits of Saddam's Winged Bulls had been vaporized with only a few percentiles of radioactive fallout having leaked into the atmosphere. Most of the fallout was clean. That was considerably better than what Saddam had planned for his Middle Eastern neighbors.

Inside the Osprey, Saxon looked down to where Dr. Jubaird Dalkimoni lay hogtied on the deck. The bomb-maker was the sole prisoner that One was taking back to Jordan with it. But Dalkimoni would not be turned over to the Marine Corps provost marshal at Drop Forge. Far from it. Saxon would make sure nobody there even knew about the prisoner. Dalkimoni's fate was to be a private matter, one that MF-1 would handle as a special favor to a good friend.

The bomb-maker didn't know it yet, but in a few days a large, containerized, climate-controlled shipping module would arrive on a Lufthansa flight into Tempelhof International Airport. The cargo would appear listed on the airline's manifest as a rare silverback gorilla destined for the internationally renowned Berlin Zoo.

The manifest would further inform customs officials that although the gorilla had been sedated for the stressful flight, the beast was still highly dangerous and not under any circumstances to be disturbed or provoked. At the airport, a team of expert animal handlers dispatched from the Berlin Zoo would arrive by truck and the cargo container be duly claimed. On the autobahn, however, the turnoff for the zoo would be bypassed and another one taken that would shortly bring the truck to BKA headquarters in Berlin. Here a grateful German cop would snap the cuffs on the savage who had killed his only joy in life.

At about the same time that this would happen, several thousand miles and several time zones away, Qusay would receive a fresh jar of fish food from one of his lackeys. He would inspect its contents and permit himself the seldomly enjoyed pleasure of a smile.

The fish would have quite a treat today, he would muse, dropping a choice tidbit from the tweezers into the tank. They seemed to relish human gonads, he would say to himself, even those such as these, still bloody from being hacked with a very dull knife from the traitorous *mahmoons* who had run from Americans rather than fight the hated Sons of Dogs.

Farther still from Berlin, yet another player in the just-ended game would sip a vodka martini and ponder the events that had recently transpired, thinking about another scheme in which his *poputchik* might prove useful. It would be wise to console him in defeat, he decided.

Setting down his glass, Soviet Premier Boris Starchinov would pick up the desk phone and order a dozen prize Siamese fighting fish delivered to Baghdad on the next available flight.